The work of forty-year-old **Michel Houellebecq**, novelist, poet, essayist, and co-founder of the influential magazine *Perpendiculaire*, has provided the catalyst for a disaffected and caustic group of young French writers who have been hailed as the most exciting literary phenomenon since the *nouveau roman*. Following the enormous success of *Whatever* – now being made into a film – Houellebecq has published a second novel, *Les particules élémentaires*, and a collection of essays, *Interventions*. He is a winner of the Grand prix national de lettres and the Prix Flore for *Whatever*.

institut français

This book is supported by the French Ministry for Foreign Affairs, as part of the Burgess Programme headed for the French Embassy in London by the Institut Français du Royaume-Uni.

Whatever
A Novel

Michel Houellebecq

Translated by Paul Hammond

This book is published with assistance from
The Arts Council of England

Library of Congress Catalog Card Number: 98–86409

A complete catalogue record for this book can be obtained from the
British Library on request

The right of Michel Houellebecq to be identified as the author of this
work has been asserted by him in accordance with the Copyright,
Designs and Patents Act 1988

First published in French as *Extension du domaine de la lutte* in 1994 by
Editions Maurice Nadeau

Copyright © Maurice Nadeau 1994
Translation copyright © 1998 Paul Hammond

This edition first published in 1998 by
Serpent's Tail, 4 Blackstock Mews, London N4
website: www.serpentstail.com

Typeset in Bembo 10 on 12pt by Intype London Ltd
Printed in Great Britain by Mackays of Chatham, plc

10 9 8 7 6 5 4 3 2

Part One

1

The night is far spent, the day is at hand: let us therefore cast off the works of darkness, and let us put on the armour of light.

– Romans XIII, 12

Friday evening I was invited to a party at a colleague from work's house. There were thirty-odd of us, all middle management aged between twenty-five and forty. At a certain moment some stupid bitch started removing her clothes. She took off her T-shirt, then her bra, then her skirt, and as she did she pulled the most incredible faces. She twirled around in her skimpy panties for a few seconds more and then, not knowing what else to do, began getting dressed again. She's a girl, what's more, who doesn't sleep with anyone. Which only underlines the absurdity of her behaviour.

After my fourth vodka I started feeling pretty groggy and had to go and stretch out on a pile of cushions behind the couch. A bit later two girls came and sat down on this same couch. Nothing beautiful about this pair, the frumps of the department in fact. They're going to have dinner together and they read books about the development of language in children, that kind of thing.

They got straight down to discussing the day's big

news, all about how one of the girls on the staff had come to work in a really mini miniskirt that barely covered her ass.

And what did they make of it all? They thought it was great. Their silhouettes came out as bizarrely enlarged Chinese shadows on the wall above me. Their voices appeared to come from on high, a bit like the Holy Ghost's. I wasn't doing at all well, that much was clear.

They went on trotting out the platitudes for a good fifteen minutes. How she had the perfect right to dress as she wished, how this had nothing to do with wanting to seduce the men, how it was just to be comfortable, to feel good about herself, etc. The last dismaying dregs of the collapse of feminism. At a certain moment I even uttered the words aloud: 'the last dismaying dregs of the collapse of feminism.' But they didn't hear me.

Me too, I'd clocked this girl. It was difficult not to. Come to that even the head of department had a hard-on.

I fell asleep before the end of the discussion, but had a horrible dream. The two frumps were arm-in-arm in the corridor that bisects the department, and they were kicking out their legs and singing at the top of their voices:

> *If I go around bare-assed*
> *It isn't to seduce you!*
> *If I show my hairy legs*
> *It's because I want to!*

The girl in the miniskirt was in a doorway, but this

time she was dressed in a long black robe, mysterious and sober. She was watching them and smiling. On her shoulders was perched a giant parrot, which represented the head of department. From time to time she stroked the feathers on its belly with a negligent but expert hand.

On waking I realized I'd thrown up on the moquette. The party was coming to an end. I concealed the vomit under a pile of cushions, then got up to try and get home. It was then that I found I'd lost my car keys.

2

Amid the Marcels

The next day but one was a Sunday. I went back to the area, but my car remained elusive. The fact was I couldn't remember where I'd parked it. Every street looked to be the one. The Rue Marcel-Sembat, Rue Marcel-Dassault . . . there were a lot of Marcels about. Rectangular buildings with people living in them. A violent feeling of identity. But where was my car?

Walking up and down these Marcels I was gradually overcome by a certain weariness in relation to cars and worldly goods. Since buying it, my Peugeot 104 had given me nothing but trouble: endless and barely comprehensible repairs, slight bumps . . . To be sure, the other drivers feign coolness, get out their nice official papers, say 'OK, no problem', but deep down they're throwing you looks full of hatred; it's most unpleasant.

And then, if you really wanted to think about it, I was getting to work on the métro; I rarely left for the weekend any more, having nowhere I wanted to go; for my holidays I was mainly opting for the organized kind, the club resort now and then. 'What good's this car?' I repeated impatiently while marching along the Rue Émile-Landrin.

It was only, however, on arriving at the Avenue Ferdi-nand-Buisson that the idea occurred to me of putting in a claim for theft. Lots of cars get stolen these days, especially in the inner suburbs; the story would be understood and readily accepted by both the insurance company and my colleagues at the office. Anyway, how was I going to say I'd lost my car? I'd pass for a practical joker, right off, a fruitcake or weirdo even; this was extremely unwise. Joking about such matters is not the done thing; this is how reputations are made, friendships formed or broken. I know life, I've grown accustomed to it. Saying you've lost your car is tantamount to being struck off the social register; let's definitely talk theft, then.

Later that evening my loneliness became tangible, pain-fully so. On the kitchen table were strewn sheets of paper, slightly spotted with the remains of a Saupiquet tuna à la catalane. These were notes relating to a story about animals; animal fiction is a literary genre like any other, maybe superior to the others; be that as it may, I write animal stories. This one was called *Dialogues Between a Cow and a Filly*; a meditation on ethics, you might say; it had been inspired by a short business trip to Brittany. Here's a key passage from it:

'Let us first consider the Breton cow: all year round she thinks of nothing but grazing, her glossy muzzle ascends and descends with impressive regularity, and no shudder of anguish comes to trouble the wistful gaze of her light-brown eyes. All that is as it ought to be, and even appears to indicate a profound existential oneness, a decidedly enviable identity between her being-in-the-world and her being-in-itself. Alas, in this instance the philosopher is found wanting, and his conclusions, while based on a correct and profound intuition, will be rendered invalid if he has not previously taken the trouble of gathering documentary evidence from the naturalist. In fact the Breton cow's nature is duplicitous. At certain times of the year (precisely determined by the inexorable functioning of genetic programming) an astonishing revolution takes place in her being. Her mooing becomes more strident, prolonged, its very harmonic texture modified to the point of recalling at times, and astonishingly so, certain groans which escape the sons of men. Her movements become more rapid, more nervous, from time to time she breaks into a trot. It is not simply her muzzle, though it seems, in its glossy regularity, conceived for reflecting the abiding presence of a mineral passivity, which contracts and twitches under the painful effect of an assuredly powerful desire.

'The key to the riddle is extremely simple, and it is that what the Breton cow desires (thus demonstrating, and she must be given credit here, her life's one desire) is, as the breeders say in their cynical parlance, "to get stuffed". And stuff her they do, more or less directly; the artificial insemination syringe can in effect, whatever the cost in certain emotional complications, take the place of the bull's penis in performing this function. In both cases the cow calms down and returns to her original state of earnest meditation, except that a few months later she will give birth to an adorable little calf. Which, let it be said in passing, means profit for the breeder.'

★

The breeder, of course, symbolized God. Moved by an irrational sympathy for the filly, he promised her, starting from the next chapter, the everlasting delight of numerous stallions, while the cow, guilty of the sin of pride, was to be gradually condemned to the dismal pleasures of artificial fertilization. The pathetic mooing of the ruminant would prove incapable of swaying the judgment of the Great Architect. A delegation of sheep, formed in solidarity, had no better luck. The God presented in this short story was not, one observes, a merciful God.

3

The problem is, it's just not enough to live according to the rules. Sure, you manage to live according to the rules. Sometimes it's tight, extremely tight, but on the whole you manage it. Your tax papers are up to date. Your bills paid on time. You never go out without your identity card (and the special little wallet for your Visa!).

Yet you haven't any friends.

The rules are complex, multiform. There's the shopping that needs doing out of working hours, the automatic dispensers where money has to be got (and where you so often have to wait). Above all there are the different payments you must make to the organizations that run different aspects of your life. You can fall ill into the bargain, which involves costs, and more formalities.

Nevertheless, some free time remains. What's to be done? How do you use your time? In dedicating yourself to helping people? But basically other people don't interest you. Listening to records? That used to be a solution, but as the years go by you have to say that music moves you less and less.

Taken in its widest sense, a spot of do-it-yourself can be a way out. But the fact is that nothing can halt the ever-increasing recurrence of those moments when your total isolation, the sensation of an all-consuming emptiness, the foreboding that your existence is nearing a painful and definitive end all combine to plunge you into a state of real suffering.

And yet you haven't always wanted to die.

You have had a life. There have been moments when you were having a life. Of course you don't remember too much about it; but there are photographs to prove it. This was probably happening round about the time of your adolescence, or just after. How great your appetite for life was, then! Existence seemed so rich in new possibilities. You might become a pop singer, go off to Venezuela.

More surprising still, you have had a childhood. Observe, now, a child of seven, playing with his little soldiers on the living room carpet. I want you to observe him closely. Since the divorce he no longer has a father. Only rarely does he see his mother, who occupies an important post in a cosmetics firm. And yet he plays with his little soldiers and the interest he takes in these representations of the world and of war seems very keen. He already lacks a bit of affection, that's for sure, but what an air he has of being interested in the world!

You too, you took an interest in the world. That was long ago. I want you to cast your mind back to then. The domain of the rules was no longer enough for you; you were unable to live any longer in the domain of the rules; so you had to enter into the domain of the struggle. I ask you to go back to that precise moment. It was long ago, no? Cast your mind back: the water was cold.

You are far from the edge, now. Oh yes! How far from the edge you are! You long believed in the existence of another shore; such is no longer the case. You go on swimming, though, and every movement you make brings you closer to drowning. You are suffocating, your lungs are on fire. The water seems colder and colder to you, more and more galling. You aren't that young any more. Now you are going to die. Don't worry. I am here. I won't let you sink. Go on with your reading.

Cast your mind back once more to your introduction to the domain of the struggle.

The pages that follow constitute a novel; I mean, a succession of anecdotes in which I am the hero. This autobiographical choice isn't one, really: in any case I have no other way out. If I don't write about what I've seen I will suffer just the same – and perhaps a bit more so. But only a bit, I insist on this. Writing brings scant relief. It retraces, it delimits. It lends a touch of coherence, the idea of a kind of realism. One stumbles around in a cruel fog, but there is the odd pointer. Chaos is no more than a few feet away. A meagre victory, in truth.

What a contrast with the absolute, miraculous power of reading! An entire life spent reading would have fulfilled my every desire; I already knew that at the age of seven. The texture of the world is painful, inadequate; unalterable, or so it seems to me. Really, I believe that an entire life spent reading would have suited me best.

Such a life has not been granted me.

★

I've just turned thirty. After a chaotic start I did very well in my studies; today I'm in middle management. Analyst-programmer in a computer software company, my salary is two and a half times the minimum wage; a tidy purchasing power, by any standards. I can expect significant advancement within my firm; unless I decide, as many do, to sign on with a client. All in all I may consider myself satisfied with my social status. On the sexual plane, on the other hand, the success is less resounding. I have had many women, but for limited periods. Lacking in looks as well as personal charm, subject to frequent bouts of depression, I don't in the least correspond to what women are usually looking for in a man. And then I've always felt a kind of slight reticence with those women who were opening their organs to me. Basically all I represented for them was a *last resort*. Which is not, you will agree, the ideal point of departure for a lasting relationship.

In fact, since my breakup with Véronique two years ago I haven't been acquainted with any women; the feeble and inconsistent attempts I've made in that direction have only resulted in predictable failure. Two years is a long time. But in reality, above all when one is working, it's no time at all. Anyone will tell you: it's no time at all.

It may be, dear reader and friend, that you are a woman yourself. Don't be alarmed, these things happen. Anyway, it changes nothing of what I have to say to you. I take the rough with the smooth.

My idea is not to try and charm you with subtle psychological observations. I have no desire to draw applause from you with my finesse and my humour. There are some authors who employ their talent in the delicate description of varying states of soul, character traits, etc. I shall not be counted among these. All that accumulation of realistic detail, with clearly differentiated characters hogging the limelight, has always seemed pure bullshit to me, I'm sorry to say. Daniel who is Hervé's friend, but who feels a certain reticence about Gérard. Paul's fantasy as embodied in Virginie, my cousin's trip to Venice . . . One could spend hours on this. Might as well watch lobsters marching up the side of an aquarium (it suffices, for that, to go to a fish restaurant). Added to which, I associate very little with other human beings.

To reach the otherwise philosophical goal I am setting myself I will need, on the contrary, to prune. To simplify. To demolish, one by one, a host of details. In this I will be aided, moreover, by the simple play of historical forces. The world is becoming more uniform before our eyes; telecommunications are improving; apartment interiors are enriched with new gadgets. Human relationships become progressively impossible, which greatly reduces the quantity of anecdote that goes to make up a life. And little by little death's countenance appears in all its glory. The third millennium augurs well.

4

Bernard, Oh Bernard

On getting back to work the following Monday, I learned that my company had just sold a specialized software program to the Ministry of Agriculture and that I'd been chosen to train them how to use it. This was announced to me by Henry La Brette (he's very proud of the 'y' of 'Henri', and his surname separated as two words). Aged thirty, like me, Henry La Brette is my immediate superior in the hierarchy. In general our relationship is marked by a veiled hostility. Hence, and as if he took personal delight in putting my nose out of joint, he immediately announced that this contract would call for a lot of travelling around: to Rouen, to La Roche-sur-Yon; I don't know where else. These trips have always been a nightmare for me and Henry La Brette knows it. I could have retorted, 'Right then, I quit.' But I didn't.

Long before the phrase became fashionable, my company developed an authentic *enterprise culture* (the creation of a logo, distribution of sweatshirts to the salaried staff, motivation seminars in Turkey). It's a top-notch enterprise, enjoying an enviable reputation in its field; a *good firm*, whichever way you look at it. I can't walk out just like that, you understand.

It's ten in the morning. I'm sitting in a cool white office, opposite a guy slightly younger than me who's just joined the firm. I think he's called Bernard. His mediocrity is distressing. He can't stop talking about money and investment: share packages, portfolios, high interest saving schemes . . . the full set. He's banking on a level of wage increase slightly higher than inflation. He bores me somewhat. I don't really manage to reply to him. His moustache twitches.

It goes quiet again once he leaves the office. We work in a totally devastated neighbourhood which looks a bit like the surface of the moon. It's somewhere in the 13th arrondissement. When you arrive by bus you'd really think World War III had happened. But no, it's only urban planning.

Our windows look out on wasteland which stretches practically as far as you can see, muddy, bristling with hoardings. A few shells of buildings. Immobile cranes. The ambience is calm and cold.

Bernard comes back. To brighten the atmosphere I tell him that it stinks in my building. People generally go for these stories of vile smells, I've observed. And it's true that coming down the stairs this morning I really did notice a pestilential odour. What's the usually so busy cleaning woman up to, then?

He says, 'It must be a dead rat somewhere.' For some reason the idea of it seems to amuse him. His moustache twitches slightly.

Poor Bernard, in a way. What can he really do with

his life? Buy CDs at the FNAC? A guy like him ought to have kids; if he had kids you'd hope he might end up getting something out of the wriggling of little Bernards. But no, he isn't even married. A dead loss.

At bottom he isn't so much to be pitied, this good Bernard, this dear Bernard. I even think he's happy – inasmuch as he can be, of course; inasmuch as he's Bernard.

5

Making Contact

Later I made an appointment at the Ministry of Agriculture with a girl called Catherine Lechardoy. The
specialized software program itself was called 'Maple'.
Aside from exuding a sugary sap the actual maple is a
tree prized in cabinet-making; it grows in certain
regions of the colder temperate zones, being particularly
widespread in Canada. The Maple program is written
in Pascal, with certain routines in C+ +. Pascal is a
seventeenth-century French writer, author of some
celebrated 'Pensées'. It is also a highly structured programming language particularly suited to the processing
of statistics, the mastery of which I'd managed to acquire
in the past. The Maple program was to be used for
paying government subsidies to the farmers, an area
Catherine Lechardoy was responsible for, at the data
processing level that is. Up till now we'd never met,
Catherine Lechardoy and I. In fine, this was a 'first
making of contact'.

In our field of computer engineering the most
interesting aspect is, without a doubt, contact with the
clients; at least this is what the company bigwigs love to
spout over a fig liqueur (I eavesdropped on their pool-

side chats a few times during the recent seminar at the Kusadasi club village).

For my part, it's always with a certain apprehension that I envisage the first contact with a new client; there are different human beings involved, organized within a certain structure, the frequentation of whom one will have to get used to; a worrying prospect. Of course experience has quickly taught me that I'm only called on to meet people who, if not exactly alike, are at least quite similar in their manners, their opinions, their tastes, their general way of approaching life. Theoretically, then, there is nothing to fear inasmuch as the professional nature of the meeting guarantees, in principle, its innocuousness. Despite that I've also had occasion to remark that human beings are often bent on making themselves conspicuous by subtle and disagreeable variations, defects, character traits and the like – doubtless with the goal of obliging their interlocutors to treat them as total individuals. Thus one person will like tennis, another will be mad on horse riding, a third will profess to playing golf. Certain higher management types are crazy about filleted herrings; others detest them. So many varied destinies, so many potential ways of doing things. Though the general framework of a 'first customer contact' is clearly circumscribed there nevertheless remains, alas, a margin of uncertainty.

As it happened Catherine Lechardoy wasn't there when I showed up in room 6017. She'd been, I was told, 'held up by a check at the central site'. I was invited to take a seat and wait for her, which I did. The conversation revolved around a bombing that had occurred the evening before on the Champs-Élysées. A bomb had been planted under a seat in a café. Two people were dead. A third had had her legs and half her face blown off; she'd be maimed and blind for life. I learned that this wasn't the first such outrage; a few days earlier a bomb had exploded in a post office near the Hôtel de Ville, blasting a fifty-year-old woman to bits. I also learned these bombs were planted by Arab terrorists who were demanding the release of other Arab terrorists, held in France for various killings.

Around five I had to leave for the police station to make a statement about the theft of my car. Catherine Lechardoy hadn't returned, and I'd barely taken part in the conversation. The making contact would take place some other day, I assumed.

The inspector who typed out my statement was around my age. Obviously of Provençal origin, he was the marrying kind. I wondered if his wife, his hypothetical kids, he himself, were happy in Paris. Wife a post office employee, kids going to nursery school? Impossible to say.

He was somewhat bitter and twisted, as you might expect. 'Thefts . . . happen every minute of the day . . . no chance . . . in any case they dump 'em straightaway . . .' I nodded sympathetically as he proceeded to utter these simple truths, drawn from his everyday experience; but I could do nothing to lighten his burden.

By the end, however, his rancour took on a slightly more positive ring, or so it seemed to me: 'Right then, be seeing you! Maybe your car'll turn up. It does happen!' He was hoping, I think, to say more on the matter; but there was nothing more to say.

6

A Second Chance

The following morning I'm told I've committed a faux pas. I should have insisted on seeing Catherine Lechardoy; my unexplained departure has been taken amiss by the Ministry of Agriculture.

I also learn – and this is a complete surprise – that since my last contract my work has not given complete satisfaction. They'd said nothing up to now, but I had been found wanting. With this Ministry of Agriculture contract I am, to some extent, being offered a second chance. My head of department assumes a tense air, pure soap opera, when telling me, 'We're at the service of the client, you know. In our line of business, alas, it's rare to get a second chance.'

I regret making this man unhappy. He is very handsome. A face at once sensual and manly, with close-cropped grey hair. White shirt of an impeccable fine weave, allowing some powerful and bronzed pecs to show through. Club tie. Natural and decisive movements, indicative of a perfect physical condition.

The only excuse I can come up with – and it seems extremely feeble to me – is that my car has just been stolen. I'm saying, then, that I'm currently grappling with a nascent psychological problem. This is when my head of department flips; the theft of my car visibly angers him. He didn't know; couldn't have guessed; now he understands. And when the moment of leave-taking arrives, standing by the door of his office, feet planted in the thick pearl-grey carpet, it's with emotion that he'll urge me 'to hang in there'.

7

Catherine, Little Catherine

The receptionist at the Ministry of Agriculture always wears a leather miniskirt; but this time I don't need her to find room 6017.

From the start Catherine Lechardoy confirms my worst fears. She's twenty-five, with a higher technical certificate in data processing, and prominent teeth; her aggressiveness is astonishing. 'Let's hope it's going to work, your software! If it's like the last one we bought from you . . . a real bastard. In the end, of course, it's not me who decides what we buy. Me, I'm just the bimbo, I'm here to clean up the shit the others leave behind . . .', etc.

I explain to her that it's not me, either, who decides what is sold. Nor what is produced. In fact I decide nothing. Neither of us decides anything. I'm just here to help her, give her some copies of the instruction manual, try and set up a teaching programme with her . . . But none of this satisfies her. Her anger is intense, her anger is deep. Now she's talking about methodology. According to her everyone in the business should conform to a rigorous methodology based on structured programming; and instead of that there is anarchy, programmes are written any old way, each person does as he likes in his little corner without considering the others, there's no agreement, there's no general project, there's no harmony. Paris is a horrible city, people don't meet, they're not even interested in their work, it's all so superficial, they all go home at six, work done or not, nobody gives a damn.

She suggests going for a coffee. I accept, obviously. An automatic machine. I haven't any change, she gives me two francs. The coffee is foul, but that doesn't stop her rant. In Paris you can drop dead right on the street, nobody gives a damn. Where she is, in the Béarn, it's different. Every weekend she goes back to her place in the Béarn. And in the evenings she takes courses at the CNAM to improve her prospects. In three years she'll maybe have her engineering diploma.

Engineer. I'm an engineer. It's vital I say something. I enquire, in a slightly strangled voice,

—Courses in what?

—Courses in management control, factor analysis, algorithmic, financial accounting.

—That must be hard work, I remark in a rather vague tone.

Yes, it's hard work, but work doesn't frighten her. In the evenings she often works in her studio flat till midnight getting her studies done. Anyway you have to fight to get anything in life, that's what she's always believed.

We go back up the stairs towards her office. 'O.K. fight, little Catherine . . .' I mournfully say to myself. She's not all that pretty. As well as prominent teeth she has lifeless hair, little eyes that burn with anger. No breasts or buttocks to speak of. God has not, in truth, been too kind to her.

I think we're going to get along very well. She has the decided air of organizing everything, running the show, all I'll have to do is come down here and give my courses. Which suits me fine; I have no wish to contradict her. I don't reckon she'll fall in love with me; I get the impression she's beyond trying it on with a man.

Around eleven a new person bursts into the office. His name is Patrick Leroy and apparently he shares the same office as Catherine. Hawaiian shirt, buttock-hugging jeans and a bunch of keys hanging from the belt, which jangle when he walks. He's a bit knackered, he informs us. He's spent the night in a jazz club with a mate, they managed to 'make it with a couple of chicks'. All in all, he's happy.

He will spend the rest of the morning on the phone. He talks in a loud voice.

During the course of the third phone call he will touch on a subject which is, in itself, extremely sad: one of their common women friends, his and the girl he's calling, has been killed in a car crash. An aggravating circumstance is that the car was driven by a third mate, whom he calls 'Old Fred'. And Old Fred himself is unscathed.

It's all, in theory, somewhat distressing, but he'll succeed in gliding over this aspect of the issue with a sort of cynical vulgarity, feet on the table and hip language. 'She was super-cool, Nathalie . . . A real goer, too. It's the pits, an absolute downer . . . You've been to the funeral? Funerals, they get to me a bit. And what's the use of 'em? Mind you, I was saying to myself, maybe for the old folk, fair does. Old Fred was there? You got to admit he's got balls, the asshole.'

I greeted lunch hour with tremendous relief.

In the afternoon I was due to see the head of the 'Computer Studies' department. I don't really know why. As far as I was concerned I had nothing to say to him.

I waited for an hour and a half in an empty, slightly gloomy office. I didn't really want to turn the light on, partly for fear of signalling my presence.

Before installing myself in this office I'd been handed a voluminous report called *Directive on the Ministry of Agriculture Data Processing Plan*. There again, I couldn't see why. The document had nothing at all to do with me. It was devoted, if the introduction was to be believed, to an *attempt at the predefinition of various archetypal scenarii, understood within a targeted objective*. The objectives, which themselves *warranted a more detailed analysis in terms of desirability*, were for instance the orientation of a politics of aid to farmers, the development of a more competitive para-agricultural sector at the European level, the redressing of the commercial balance in the realm of fresh products . . . I quickly leafed through the opus, underlining the more amusing phrases in pencil: *The strategic level consists in the realization of a system of global information promulgated by the integration of diversified heterogeneous sub-systems*. Or indeed: *It appears urgent to validate a canonic relational model within an organizational dynamic leading in the medium term to a database-oriented object*. A secretary finally appeared to advise me that the meeting was taking longer than expected and that it would unfortunately be impossible for her boss to receive me today.

So I took myself off home. As long as they're paying me, ha ha!

I spotted a strange graffito in the Sèvres–Babylon métro station: 'God wanted there to be inequality, not injustice', the inscription said. I mused on who the person so well informed about God's designs might be.

8

In general I see nobody at the weekends. I stay home, do a bit of tidying. I get gently depressed.

This Saturday however, between eight and eleven, a social moment is in the offing. I am to eat with a priest friend in a Mexican restaurant. The restaurant is good; on that front, no problem. But is my friend still my friend?

We did our studies together: we were twenty, just kids really. Now we're thirty. Once he'd got his engineer's diploma he went off to the seminary, he changed course. Today he's a parish priest in Vitry. It isn't an easy parish.

I eat a red bean taco and Jean-Pierre Buvet talks to me about sexuality. According to him the interest our society pretends to show in eroticism (through advertising magazines, the media in general) is completely artificial. Most people, in fact, are quickly bored by the subject, but they pretend the opposite out of a bizarre inverted hypocrisy.

He gets to his main thesis. Our civilization, he says, suffers from vital exhaustion. In the century of Louis XIV, when the appetite for living was great, official culture placed the accent on the negation of pleasure and of the flesh; repeated insistently that mundane life can offer only imperfect joys, that the only true source of happiness was in God. Such a discourse, he asserts, would no longer be tolerated today. We need adventure and eroticism because we need to hear ourselves repeat that life is marvellous and exciting; and it's abundantly clear that we rather doubt this.

I get the impression he considers me a fitting symbol of this vital exhaustion. No sex drive, no ambition; no real interests, either. I don't know what to say to him: I get the impression everybody's a bit like that. I consider myself a normal kind of guy. Well, perhaps not completely, but who is completely, huh? Eighty per cent normal, let's say.

For something to say in the meantime I casually observe that these days everybody is bound, at one moment or another in his life, to have the feeling of being a failure. We are agreed on that.

The conversation stalls. I nibble my caramelized vermicelli. He advises me to find God again, or go into psychoanalysis; I give a start at the comparison. He's interested in my case, he explains; he seems to think I'm in a bad way. I'm alone, much too alone; it isn't natural, according to him.

We have a brandy. He lays his cards on the table. As far as he's concerned Jesus is the answer; the wellspring of life. Of a rich and active life. 'You must accept your divine nature!' he exclaims; the next table turns round. I feel a little tired; I get the impression we're reaching an impasse. I smile, just in case. I haven't got too many friends, I don't want to lose this one. 'You must accept your divine nature,' he repeats more softly; I promise I'll make an effort. I add a few words, I force myself to re-establish a consensus.

Next, a coffee, and each to his home. In the end it was a pleasant evening.

9

Six persons are presently gathered around a rather nice oval table, probably in fake mahogany. The curtains, of a sombre green, are drawn; you'd think you were in a small drawing room. I suddenly have the feeling that the meeting is going to last all morning.

The first Ministry of Agriculture representative has blue eyes. He is young, has little round glasses, he must have still been a student up till a short time ago. Despite his youth he gives a remarkable impression of seriousness. He will take notes all morning, sometimes at the most unexpected moments. Here is a leader of men, or at least a future leader.

The second Ministry representative is a middle-aged man with a fringe of beard, like the fearsome tutors in *The Famous Five*. He seems to exert a great influence on Catherine Lechardoy, who is seated at his side. He is a theoretician. His interventions will be so many calls to order concerning the importance of methodology and, more generally, of reflection prior to action. At this juncture I don't see why: the software is already paid for, there's no more need to reflect, but I refrain from saying so. I immediately get the feeling he doesn't like me. How can I gain his love? I decide that on several occasions in the morning I will support his interventions with a slightly stupid expression of admiration, as if he'd suddenly opened up astonishing perspectives for me, full of wisdom and breadth. He must, in the normal course of things, conclude from this that I am a young man of goodwill, ready to engage myself under his orders in the proper direction.

The third Ministry representative is Catherine Lechardoy. The poor thing has a slightly sad air this morning; all her recent combativeness seems to have left her. Her ugly little face is glum, she regularly wipes her glasses. I even wonder if she hasn't been crying; I can just picture her breaking into sobs in the morning as she gets dressed, all alone.

The fourth Ministry representative is a kind of caricature of the rural socialist. He wears boots and a parka, as if he was just back from a field trip; he has a thick beard and smokes a pipe; I wouldn't like to be his son. In front of him on the table he has ostentatiously placed a book called *Cheesemaking and the Challenge of New Technologies*. I can't work out what he's doing there, he obviously knows nothing about the subject under discussion; perhaps he's a trade union representative. Whatever the truth of it, he seems to have set himself the goal of making the atmosphere more tense and of provoking conflict by means of repetitive remarks about 'the uselessness of these meetings which never get anywhere', or else 'these software packages chosen in a Ministry office which never correspond to the real needs of the chaps on the ground'.

Opposite him is a guy from my company who responds tirelessly to his objections – in a very clumsy way, in my opinion – by pretending to believe that the other man is deliberately exaggerating, even that the whole thing is pure pleasantry. He is one of my superiors in the hierarchy; I think his name is Norbert Lejailly. I didn't know he'd be here, and I can't say I'm overjoyed by his presence. This man has the features and the behaviour of a pig. He seizes the least opportunity to laugh long and loud. When he isn't laughing he slowly rubs his hands together. He is podgy, even obese, and his self-satisfaction, which nothing solid would seem to support, is absolutely unbearable to me. But this morning I feel really rather good, and on two occasions I will even laugh with him, in echo of his witticisms.

During the morning a seventh person will make periodic appearances, intended to jolly along this meeting of minds. He is the head of the Ministry of Agriculture 'Computer Studies' section, the one I missed the other day. This individual seems to have given himself the mission of embodying an exaggerated version of the young and dynamic boss. In this he's streets ahead of anything I've had occasion to observe up till now. His shirt is open, as if he hadn't quite had the time to button it up, and his tie flies off to one side as if caught in a slipstream. He doesn't walk down the corridors, he glides. If he could fly, he would. His face is shining, his hair disordered and damp as if he'd come straight from the swimming pool.

On his first entrance he sees us, me and my boss. In a flash he's standing by us, without me figuring out how. He must have covered the ten metres in less than five seconds, in any event he was too fast for me.

He places his hand on my shoulder and speaks to

me in a gentle voice, saying how much he's sorry for making me wait for nothing the other day; I give him an angelic smile, tell him it's of no importance, that I understand and that I know that sooner or later the meeting will take place. I am being sincere. It is a very tender moment. He is leaning towards me and me alone. You'd think we were two lovers whom life had just reunited after a long separation.

He will make two other appearances during the morning, but each time he'll remain at the door, addressing himself solely to the young guy in glasses. Each time he begins by excusing himself for disturbing us with an enchanting smile; he stays at the door, hanging on the jamb, balancing on one leg as if the inner tension that drives him prevented him from standing upright for too long.

Of the meeting itself I retain but few memories; in any case nothing concrete was decided, except for in the last quarter of an hour, very quickly, just before going to lunch, when a training timetable for the provinces was drawn up. I am directly concerned, since it's me who will have to do the travelling around; so I hastily take note of the dates and places booked on a piece of paper which I will, as it happens, mislay that same evening.

The whole thing will be explained to me again next day in the course of a *briefing* with the theoretician. Thus I learn that a sophisticated three-tier system of training has been set up by the Ministry (therefore by him, if I understand things correctly). It is a question of how best to respond to the needs of the users by means of a complementary, but organically independent, package of training programmes. All this clearly bears the stamp of a subtle mind.

In real terms I will be involved in a tour that will take me firstly to Rouen for a duration of two weeks, then to Dijon for a week, and lastly to La Roche-sur-Yon for four days. I will leave on the first of December and be home again for Christmas, so as to enable me to 'spend the holidays with my family'. The human aspect has not been forgotten, then. How splendid.

I also learn – and it's a surprise – that I will not be alone in undertaking these training programmes. In effect my company has decided to send two people. We will work in tandem. For twenty-five minutes, and in an agonizing silence, the theoretician points out the advantages and the disadvantages of the tandem training. Finally, *in extremis*, the advantages seem to carry the day.

I am completely in the dark about the identity of the second person who is required to accompany me. It's probably someone I know. In any event nobody has seen fit to notify me.

Cleverly taking advantage of an unrelated remark he has just made, the theoretician makes the observation that it is a real pity this second person (whose identity will remain a mystery until the last minute) is not there, and that nobody thought it wise to invite him. Pushing on with his argument, he contrives to implicitly suggest that in these conditions my own presence is itself just as useless, or at very least of limited use. Which is precisely what I'm thinking.

10

The Degrees of Freedom According to J.-Y. Fréhaut

Afterwards, I go back to company headquarters. A good reception awaits me there; I have, it seems, succeeded in re-establishing my standing in the company.

My head of department takes me to one side; he reveals to me the importance of this contract. He knows I'm a solid young man. He devotes a few words, of a bitter realism, to the theft of my car. This is verily a conversation between men, next to the automatic hot drinks machine. In him I discern a true professional in the management of human resources; I'm putty in his hands. He seems ever more handsome to me.

Later that afternoon I will attend the farewell drink for Jean-Yves Fréhaut. A much-valued asset is leaving the firm, the head of department affirms; a technician of the highest calibre. In his future career he will doubtless know successes at least as great as those which have marked this one; this is the very least he wishes him. And may he drop by whenever he likes, to drain the cup of friendship! Like a first love, a first job, he concludes in a ribald tone, is something that's hard to forget. I wonder right then if he hasn't drunk too much.

Brief applause. Some movement is registered around J.-Y. Fréhaut; he turns on his heel with a satisfied air. I know this young man slightly; we arrived at the firm at the same time, three years ago; we used to share the same office. We'd talked about civilization one time. He claimed – and in a sense he truly believed it – that the increase in the flow of information within society was in itself a good thing. That freedom was nothing other than the possibility of establishing various interconnections between individuals, projects, organizations, services. According to him the maximum amount of freedom coincided with the maximum amount of potential choice. In a metaphor borrowed from the mechanics of solids, he called these choices degrees of freedom.

We were, I remember, sitting near the central processing unit. The air conditioning was emitting a slight hum. He was comparing society to a brain, as it were, and its individuals to so many cerebral cells for which it is, in effect, desirable to establish the maximum number of interconnections. But the analogy stopped there. For this was a liberal, and he was scarcely a partisan of what is so necessary to the brain: a unifying project.

His own life, I would subsequently learn, was functional in the extreme. He was living in a studio flat in the 15th arrondissement. The heating was included in the rent. He barely did more than sleep there, since he was in fact working a lot – and often, outside of working time, he was reading *Micro-Systèmes*. The famous degrees of freedom consisted, as far as he was concerned, in choosing his dinner by Minitel (he was a subscriber to this service, new at the time, which guaranteed the delivery of hot food at a given hour and with relatively little delay).

I liked to think of him of an evening composing his menu, using the Minitel which sat on the left corner of his desk. I used to tease him about the telephone hot-lines; but in reality I'm sure he was a virgin.

He was happy in a sense. He took himself to be, and rightly so, a participant in the telecommunications revolution. He actually did live each increase in computer power, each step towards the globalization of the network, as a personal victory. He voted socialist. And, funnily enough, he adored Gauguin.

11

I was never to see Jean-Yves Fréhaut again. And anyway, why would I have? Basically we'd never really *clicked*. In any event people rarely *see each other again* these days, even in cases where the relationship begins in an atmosphere of enthusiasm. Sometimes breathless conversations take place, touching on the general aspects of life; sometimes, too, a carnal embrace comes about. Sure, you exchange telephone numbers but, generally speaking, you rarely call again. And even when you do call and meet up, disillusionment and disenchantment rapidly take over from the initial enthusiasm. Believe me, I know life; it's all perfectly cut and dried.

This progressive effacement of human relationships is not without certain problems for the novel. How, in point of fact, would one handle the narration of those unbridled passions, stretching over many years, and at times making their effect felt on several generations? We're a long way from *Wuthering Heights*, to say the least. The novel form is not conceived for depicting indifference or nothingness; a flatter, more terse and dreary discourse would need to be invented.

If human relations become progressively impossible this is due, precisely, to the multiplying of those degrees of freedom of which Jean-Yves Fréhaut declared himself the enthusiastic prophet. He himself had never known any *intimate relationship*, of that I'm sure; his state of freedom was extreme. There is no acrimony in what I say. Here was, as I've mentioned, a happy man; that said, I don't envy him his happiness.

The species of information technology thinker to which Jean-Yves Fréhaut belonged is less rare than you'd think. In every average-sized company you can find one, occasionally two. Besides, most people vaguely admit that every relationship, in particular every human relationship, is *reduced* to an exchange of information (if of course you include in the notion of information messages of a non-neutral, that is, gratifying or punitive, nature). Under these conditions it doesn't take long for a thinker on information technology to be transformed into a thinker on social evolution. His discourse will often be brilliant, and hence convincing; the affective dimension may even be built into it.

The next day – again on the occasion of a farewell drink, but this time at the Ministry of Agriculture – I had occasion to discuss things with the theoretician, flanked as usual by Catherine Lechardoy. He himself had never met Jean-Yves Fréhaut, and would have no occasion to do so. I imagine that in a hypothetical meeting the intellectual exchange would have been courteous, yet of a high level. Doubtless they'd have arrived at a consensus on certain values such as freedom, transparency and the necessity of establishing a system of generalized transactions subsuming the totality of social activities.

The object of this moment of conviviality was to fête

the retirement of a small man of some sixty years with grey hair and thick glasses. The staff had clubbed together to buy him a fishing rod – a high-performance Japanese model, with three-speed reel and range modifiable by simple finger pressure – but he didn't know that yet. He was staying well in sight beside the bottles of champagne. People were coming up and giving him a friendly pat on the back, even evoking a shared memory.

Next, the head of the 'Computer Studies' department began to speak. It was an impossible task, he announced right away, to summarize in a few words thirty years of a career devoted entirely to agricultural computing. Louis Lindon, he recalled, had known the heroic days of computerization: punched cards! power cuts! magnetic drums! With each exclamation he spread his arms wide, as if bidding those present to cast their minds back to that far-distant time.

The interested party was smiling with a knowing air, chewing his moustache in a most unpleasant manner. But on the whole he behaved correctly.

Louis Lindon, the head of department concluded warmly, had put his stamp on agricultural computing. Without him the Ministry of Agriculture computer system would not be what it was today. And that was something none of his present and even future colleagues (his voice became slightly more tremulous) could ever forget.

There were thirty seconds or so of warm applause. A young girl chosen from among the fairest handed the future pensioner his fishing rod. He brandished it timidly at the end of his arm. This was the signal for heading for the buffet. The head of department went up to Louis Lindon and, putting an arm around his shoulders, slow-marched him away to exchange a few extra tender and heartfelt words.

This was the moment the theoretician chose to confide to me that, even so, Lindon belonged to another generation of computing. He programmed without real method, partly by intuition; he'd had persistent difficulty adapting to the principles of functional analysis; the concepts of the *Merise* method had largely passed him by. All the programmes of which he was the author had had to be rewritten, in fact; for the last two years he'd not been given very much to do, he was more or less put out to grass. Lindon's personal qualities, he added warmly, were not at all in question. Things simply change, it's normal.

Having dispatched Louis Lindon to the mists of time the theoretician could move on to his favourite theme: according to him the production and circulation of information ought to undergo the same mutation that the production and circulation of commodities had known: the transition from the artisanal stage to the industrial stage. In matters of the production of information, he stated acrimoniously, we were still far from *zero default*: redundancy and imprecision were more often than not the rule. Since they were insufficiently developed, the information distribution networks remained marked by approximation and anachronism (because of this, he angrily pointed out, Telecom was still distributing phone directories on paper!). Thank God the young were clamouring for more and better information; thank God they were showing themselves to be increasingly exigent about response time; but the road that would lead to a perfectly informed, perfectly transparent and communicating society was still long.

He developed still other ideas; Catherine Lechardoy was at his side. From time to time she acquiesced with a 'Yes, that's very important.' She had red on her mouth and blue on her eyes. Her skirt reached halfway down her thighs and her tights were black. I suddenly realized that she must buy panties, maybe even g-strings; the hubbub in the room became slightly more animated. I imagined her in Galeries Lafayette choosing a Brazilian tanga in scarlet lace; I felt invaded by an aching sense of compassion.

At that moment a colleague came up to the theoretician. Turning away from us slightly, each man offered the other a panatella. Catherine Lechardoy and I remained facing each other. A distinct silence fell. Then, seeking a way out, she proceeded to talk about the bringing into line of work procedures between the servicing company and the Ministry – that's to say, between the two of us. She was still standing right beside me – our bodies were separated by a gap of thirty centimetres at most. At a certain moment, and with a clearly involuntary gesture, she lightly rubbed the lapel of my jacket between her fingers.

I felt no desire for Catherine Lechardoy; I hadn't the slightest wish to *shaft* her. She was looking at me and smiling, drinking Crémant, trying her hardest to be brave; nevertheless I knew she really needed to be *shafted*. That hole she had at the base of her belly must appear so useless to her; a prick can always be cut off, but how do you forget the emptiness of a vagina? Her situation appeared desperate, and my tie was beginning to choke me slightly. After my third glass I came close to suggesting we leave together, go and fuck in some office; on the desk or on the carpet, it didn't matter; I was feeling up to making the necessary gestures. But I kept my mouth shut; and anyway I don't think she'd have accepted; or else I'd have first had to put my arm around her waist, say she was beautiful, brush her lips in a tender kiss. There was no way out, for sure. I briefly excused myself and went to throw up in the toilets.

On my return the theoretician was at her side and she was listening to him docilely. She'd managed, in short, to regain control; perhaps it was all to the good, for her.

12

This retirement drink was to constitute the derisory apogee of my relations with the Ministry of Agriculture. I had gathered together all the necessary material for preparing my courses; we'd barely be seeing each other again; I still had a week before leaving for Rouen.

A gloomy week. We were at the end of November, a time which is commonly taken to be gloom itself. For me it seemed normal that, for want of more tangible events, changes in the weather would assume a certain place in my life; besides, old people can talk about nothing else, they say.

I've lived so little that I tend to imagine I'm not going to die; it seems improbable that human existence can be reduced to so little; one imagines, in spite of oneself, that sooner or later something is bound to happen. A big mistake. A life can just as well be both empty and short. The days slip by indifferently, leaving neither trace nor memory; and then all of a sudden they stop.

At times, too, I've had the impression that I'd manage to feel quite at home in a life of vacuity. That the relatively painless boredom would enable me to go on making the usual gestures of life. Another big mistake. Prolonged boredom is not tenable as a position: sooner or later it is transformed into feelings that are acutely more painful, of true pain; this is precisely what's happening to me.

Maybe, I tell myself, this tour of the provinces is going *to alter my ideas*. Doubtless in a negative sense, but it's going *to alter my ideas*; at least there will be a change of direction, a shake-up.

Part Two

1

At the approaches to the narrows of Bab-el-Mandel, beneath the ambiguous and immutable surface of the sea, huge and irregularly spaced coral reefs are hidden which represent a real danger to navigation. They are barely perceptible except for a reddish bloom, a slightly different tinge to the water. And if the occasional traveller should call to mind the extraordinary density of the shark population which characterizes this area of the Red Sea (it has some two thousand sharks per square kilometre, if my memory serves me correct), then it will be readily understood if, despite the overwhelming and almost unreal heat that makes the surrounding air quiver with a viscous bubbling, he feels a slight shudder at the approaches to the narrows of Bab-el-Mandel.

Fortunately, because of the odd way the sky reacts, the weather is always fine, excessively fine, and the horizon never deviates from an overheated and blinding whiteness which can also be observed in metal foundries during the third phase of treating the iron ore (I am speaking of that moment when there blossoms forth, as if suspended in the atmosphere and bizarrely at one with its intrinsic nature, the newly-formed flow of molten steel). That is why most pilots clear this obstacle without let or hindrance and are soon sailing in silence through the calm, iridescent and limpid waters of the Gulf of Aden.

Sometimes, though, such things happen, occur for real. It's Monday morning, the first of December; it's cold and I am waiting for Tisserand by the departure gate of the train for Rouen; we're in the Gare Saint-Lazare; I'm getting more and more cold and more and more pissed off. Tisserand arrives at the last minute; we're going to have difficulty finding seats. Unless he's got himself a first-class ticket; that would be quite his style.

I might have formed a *tandem* with four or five other people from my company, and in the end it's come down to Tisserand. I'm not wildly excited about it. He, on the other hand, declares himself delighted. 'We make a terrific team you and me,' he promptly declares, 'I reckon things'll work out just great.' He describes a sort of rotating movement with his hands, as if to symbolize our future mutual understanding.

I already know this young man; we've chatted many a time around the hot drinks machine. He generally told *dirty stories*; I have the feeling this tour of the provinces is going to be grim.

Moments later the train is moving. We install ourselves in the midst of a group of garrulous students who seem to belong to a business school. I settle myself near the window to escape the surrounding noise, at least a bit. From his briefcase Tisserand extracts various coloured brochures dealing with accounting software; these have nothing to do with the training we're going to give. I hazard the remark. He interjects vaguely, 'Ah yes,

Maple, that's good too,' then goes back to his mono-logue. Where the technical aspects are concerned I've the impression he's counting on me one hundred per cent.

He's wearing a splendid suit with a red, yellow and green pattern – a bit medieval tapestry, you'd say. He also has a fancy handkerchief which sticks out of his jacket pocket, 'Trip to the Planet Mars' style, and a matching tie. His whole outfit evokes the ultra-dynamic business management type, not without humour. As for me, I'm dressed in a quilted parka and 'Weekend in the Heb-rides' chunky pullover. I imagine that in the play of roles that's gradually falling into place I represent the 'systems man', the competent but slightly oafish technician who doesn't have the time to worry about his appearance and is completely incapable of dialoguing with the user. That suits me fine. He's right, we make a good team.

In getting all his brochures out, I ask myself if he isn't trying to attract the attention of the young girl sitting on his left – a student at the business school, and very pretty. His discourse would only seem, then, superficially directed at me. I permit myself a glance or two at the landscape. Day is beginning to break. The sun appears, blood red, terribly red above the dark green grass, above the mist-shrouded ponds. Small clusters of houses smoke far away in the valley. The sight is magnificent, a little scary. Tisserand isn't interested by it. Instead, he's trying to catch the glance of the student on his left. The problem with Raphaël Tisserand – the foundation of his personality, indeed – is that he is extremely ugly. So ugly that his appearance repels women, and he never gets to sleep with them. He tries though, he tries with all his might, but it doesn't work. They simply want nothing to do with him.

His body is nonetheless close to normal. Vaguely Mediterranean in type, he is certainly rather fat; 'stocky', as they say; added to which his baldness is coming along nicely. Fine, all this could still be arranged; but what isn't fine is his face. He has the exact appearance of a buffalo toad – thick, gross, heavy, deformed features, the very opposite of handsome. His shiny acned skin seems to permanently exude a greasy fluid. He wears bifocal glasses, because he's extremely short-sighted to boot – yet if he had contact lenses it wouldn't change anything, I'm afraid. What's more, his conversation lacks finesse, fantasy, humour; he has absolutely no *charm* (charm is a quality which can sometimes substitute for physical beauty – at least in men; anyway, one often says 'He has loads of charm', or 'The most important thing is charm'; that's what one says). Given all this, he is obviously terribly frustrated; but what can I do about it? So I gaze out at the landscape.

A bit later he engages the student in conversation. We skirt the Seine, scarlet, completely drowned in the rays of the rising sun – one would really think the river gorged with blood.

Around nine we arrive in Rouen. The student says her goodbyes to Tisserand – she refuses to give him her telephone number of course. For a few minutes he will feel a certain despondency; it's going to be me who has to find a bus.

The Departmental Headquarters for Agriculture building is evil-looking and we are late. Here, work begins at eight – this, I will learn, is often the case in the provinces. The training session gets going immediately. Tisserand is first to speak; he introduces himself, introduces me, introduces our company. After that I assume he'll introduce the computer, the integrated software, their advantages. He could also introduce the course, the work method we are going to follow, lots of things. All this should take us to around midday, no problem, especially if there's a good old-fashioned coffee-break. I take off my parka, place a few sheets of paper before me.

The audience is made up of fifteen or so people; there are some secretaries and middle management, some technicians I imagine – they have the look of technicians. They don't seem particularly hostile, or particularly interested in computers either – and yet, I say to myself, computers are going to change their lives.

I spot straightaway where the danger lies: an extremely young guy in glasses, tall, lanky and lithe. He has installed himself at the back so he can watch everybody; I silently dub him 'the Serpent', but in actual fact he will introduce himself to us after the coffee-break by the name of Schnäbele. Here in the making is the future boss of the computer service, and he has a very satisfied air about it. Sitting at his side is a guy of fifty-odd, extremely well-built, unpleasant-looking, with a fringe of red beard. He must be an ex-sergeant-major, or something of the sort. He has a beady eye – Indo-china, I imagine – which he will keep trained on me for ages, as if summoning me to explain the reason for my presence. He seems devoted body and soul to the Serpent, his boss. He has something of the mastiff about him – the kind of dog which never lets go its bite, in any event.

All too soon the Serpent will fire off various questions whose object is to throw Tisserand, make him look incompetent. Tisserand is incompetent, this is a fact, but he's come across such types before. He's a professional. He will have no difficulty in parrying the various attacks, now dodging with grace, now promising to return to them at some later point in the course. He will sometimes even succeed in suggesting that the question might indeed have had a point at an earlier period in the development of computers, but that it has now been rendered meaningless.

At midday we are interrupted by the strident and disagreeable ringing of a bell. Schnäbele sidles up to us: 'Do we eat together?' The question admits of no reply.

He tells us that, sorry, he has a few little things to do before lunch. But we can go with him, like that he can 'show us round the place'. He leads us down the corridors; his acolyte follows, two paces behind. Tisserand manages to get it across to me that he'd have 'preferred to eat with the two cuties in the third row'. He's already spotted the female prey in the audience, then; it was almost inevitable, but all the same I find it a little disturbing.

We go into Schnäbele's office. The acolyte remains rooted on the threshold in an attitude of expectancy; he is mounting guard to some extent. The room is big, even very big for such a young executive, and I instantly surmise that it's only to show us it that he's brought us here, since he does nothing – he contents himself with tapping nervously on his telephone. I sink down into an armchair in front of the desk, Tisserand immediately following suit. The other jerk chimes in with 'Sure, take a seat.' The same second a secretary comes through a door off to one side. She approaches the desk respectfully. She is a rather old woman with glasses. In her open hands she holds a file of letters awaiting signature. Here at last, I say to myself, is the reason for this whole performance.

Schnäbele performs his role most impressively. Before signing the first document he goes through it at length, with tremendous gravity. He singles out a phrase which is 'somewhat unfortunate at the syntactical level.' The secretary, confused: 'I can do it again, Sir'; and he, the great lord: 'No, no, it'll be fine.'

The fastidious ceremony is repeated for a second document, then for a third. I start to feel hungry. I get up to examine the photos hanging on the wall. They are amateur photos, printed and framed with care. They appear to represent geysers, ice formations, things of the sort. I imagine he's printed them himself after his holidays in Iceland – a Nouvelles Frontières tour, in all likelihood. But he has been prodigal with the solarizations, star-filter effects and I don't know what else besides, to such an extent that one recognizes practically nothing and the general effect is exceedingly ugly.

Seeing my interest, he approaches and says:

—It's Iceland . . . It's really pretty, I find.

—Ah, I reply.

We're finally going to eat. Schnäbele goes on ahead of us down the corridors, commenting on the organization of the offices and the 'spatial layout', exactly as if he'd just acquired the whole place. Now and again, at the moment of making a right-hand turn, he circles my shoulder with his arm – yet without, happily, touching me. He walks quickly and Tisserand, with his little legs, is hard pressed to keep up – I hear him puffing at my side. Two paces behind us the acolyte brings up the rear, as if to forestall an eventual surprise attack.

The meal will prove interminable. To begin with all goes well, Schnäbele talks about himself. He informs us once more that at twenty-five he is already head of the computer service, or at least on the way to being so in the near future. He will remind us of his age three times between the hors-d'oeuvre and the main course: twenty-five.

Next he wants to know about our 'training', probably to assure himself that it's inferior to his own. (He himself is an IGREF, and has the air of being proud of it; I don't know what this is but will subsequently learn that IGREFs are a particular kind of higher civil servant who are only to be found in organizations depending on the Ministry of Agriculture – a bit like the graduates of the École Nationale d'Administration, but less qualified all the same.) In this respect Tisserand gives him complete satisfaction: he claims to have been to the École Supérieure de Commerce in Bastia, or something of the kind, which is scarcely believable. I chew on my steak béarnaise, pretending not to have heard the question. The sergeant-major fixes me with his beady eye, and for a moment I wonder if he isn't going to start screaming 'Answer when you're spoken to!'; I turn my head squarely in the other direction. Finally Tisserand replies in my place. He presents me as a 'systems engineer'. As if to give credence to the idea I utter a few phrases about Scandinavian norms and network changeovers; Schnäbele, on the defensive, twists in his seat; I go to get myself a crème caramel.

The afternoon will be devoted to practical work on the computer. It's then that I move into action: while Tisserand continues with his explanations I pass among the groups to check that everybody is managing to follow, to accomplish the set exercises. I handle it very well; but then that's my job.

I am often called upon by the two cuties; they are secretaries, and apparently this is the first time they've been in front of a computer console. So they're a bit panicky and, what's more, rightly so. But each time I go over to them Tisserand intervenes, without hesitating to interrupt his explanation. It's mainly one of the two who attracts him, I get the feeling; and it's true that she is ravishing, fleshy, very sexy; she wears a bustier of black lace and her breasts move slightly beneath the material. Alas, each time he goes up to the poor little secretary her face contorts in an expression of involuntary repulsion, of disgust, one might almost say. It was bound to happen.

At five another bell rings out. The students gather up their things, prepare to leave; but Schnäbele makes for us: the venomous soul has, it seems, another card up his sleeve. He immediately tries to buttonhole me with an opening remark: 'If anything, this is a question, I'd say, for a systems man like you.' Then he explains his problem to me: should he or shouldn't he buy a thyratron inverter to stabilize the incoming voltage of the current feeding the server network? He's heard conflicting opinions on the subject. I know absolutely nothing about it and am about to tell him so. But Tisserand, clearly in top form, beats me to it: a study has just been published on the subject, he audaciously affirms; the conclusions are obvious: above a certain ratio of work to machine the inverter rapidly pays its way, in less than three years in any event. Unfortunately he doesn't have the study on him, or even the reference; but he promises to send him a photocopy on returning to Paris.

A palpable hit. Schnäbele backs away, completely brow-beaten; he even goes so far as to wish us a pleasant evening.

The evening will firstly consist in finding a hotel. On Tisserand's initiative we book into the 'Armes Cauchoises'. A nice hotel, a very nice hotel; and anyway our expenses are reimbursed, right?

Next he wants to have an apéritif. By all means!

In the café he chooses a table not far from two girls. He sits down, the girls get up and go. No doubt about it, the plan is perfectly synchronized. Bravo girls, bravo!

In desperation he orders a Martini; I content myself with a beer. I feel rather nervous; I don't stop smoking, I literally light one cigarette after another.

He tells me he's just signed on with a gym to lose a bit of weight, 'and also to score, of course.' An excellent idea, I'm not against it.

I realize I'm smoking more and more; I must be on at least four packs a day. Smoking cigarettes has become the only element of real freedom in my life. The only act to which I tenaciously cling with my whole being. My one ambition.

Tisserand next broaches a favourite theme of his, namely that 'It's us guys, the computer experts, we're the kings.' I suppose by that he means a high salary, a certain professional status, a great facility for changing jobs. And OK, within these limits he isn't wrong. We are the kings.

He expands on his idea; I open my fifth pack of Camels. Shortly afterwards he finishes his Martini; he wants to return to the hotel to change for dinner. Right then, fine, let's go for it.

I wait for him in the lounge while watching television. There's something on about student demonstrations. One of these, in Paris, has assumed enormous proportions: according to the journalists there were at least three hundred thousand people on the streets. It was supposed to be a non-violent demonstration, more like a big party. And like all non-violent demonstrations it turned nasty, a student has lost an eye, a CRS policeman has had a hand torn off, etc.

The day after this huge demonstration a march has taken place in Paris to protest against 'police brutality'. It has passed off in an atmosphere 'of overwhelming dignity' reports the commentator, who is clearly on the students' side. All this dignity gets on my nerves; I change channel and chance on a sexy pop promo. Finally I switch off.

Tisserand returns; he's put on a sort of evening shell-suit, black and gold, which makes him look rather like a scarab beetle. Right then, let's go for it.

★

As to the restaurant, we go at my insistence to The Flunch. It's a place where you can eat chips with an unlimited quantity of mayonnaise (all you do is scoop as much mayonnaise as you want from a giant bucket); I'll be happy, come to that, with a plate of chips drowned in mayonnaise, and a beer. Tisserand himself immediately orders a couscous royal and a bottle of Sidi Brahim. After the second glass of wine he begins eyeing up the waitresses, the customers, anybody. Sad young man. Sad, sad young man. I'm well aware of why he basically likes my company so much: it's because I never speak of my girlfriends. I never make a big thing of my female conquests. And so he feels justified in supposing (rightly, as it happens) that for one reason or another I don't have a sex life; and for him that's one less burden, a slight easing of his own martyrdom. I remember being present at a distressing scene the day Tisserand was introduced to Thomassen, who'd just joined our firm. Thomassen is Swedish in origin; he is extremely tall (a bit over six foot three, I reckon), superbly well-proportioned, and his face is incredibly handsome, sunny and radiant; you really have the impression of being in the presence of a superman, a demigod.

Thomassen first shook my hand, then went over to Tisserand. Tisserand got up and realized that, standing, the other man was a good fifteen inches taller than him. He abruptly sat down, his face went bright red, I even thought for a moment that he was going to go for Thomassen's throat; it was painful to see.

Later I made a number of trips to the provinces with Thomassen – for training sessions, the usual sort of thing. We got on really well. I've remarked it time and again: exceptionally beautiful people are often modest, gentle, affable, considerate. They have great difficulty in making friends, at least among men. They're forced to make a constant effort to try and make you forget their superiority, be it ever so little.

Tisserand, thank God, has never been called on to make a trip with Thomassen. But each time a group of training sessions is being organized I know he thinks about it, and that he has a lot of sleepless nights.

After the meal he wants to go for a drink in a 'friendly café'. Wonderful.

I follow just behind, and I have to say this time his choice turns out to be excellent: we go into a kind of huge vaulted cellar, with old, obviously authentic beams. Small wooden tables, lit with candles, are dotted all over the place. A fire burns in an immense fireplace at the end of the room. The whole thing makes for an atmosphere of happy improvization, of congenial disorder.

We sit down. He orders a bourbon and water, I stick to beer. I look about me and say to myself that this time this is it, this is perhaps the journey's end for my luckless companion. We're in a student café, everyone's happy, everybody wants to have fun. There are lots of tables with two or three young women at them, there are even some girls alone at the bar.

I watch Tisserand while assuming my most engaging air. The young men and women in the café touch each other. The women push back their hair with a graceful gesture. They cross their legs, await the occasion to burst into laughter. In short, they've having fun. Now's the time to score, right here and now, in this place that lends itself so perfectly.

He raises his eyes from his drink and, from behind his glasses, fixes his gaze on me. And I remark that he's run out of steam. He can't go on, he has no more appetite for the fray, he's had it up to here. He looks at me, his face trembles a little. Doubtless it's the alcohol, he drank too much wine at dinner, the jerk. I wonder if he isn't going to break into sobs, recount the stations of his particular cross to me; I feel him capable of something of the sort; the lenses of his glasses are slightly fogged with tears.

It's not a problem, I can handle it, listen to the lot, carry him back to the hotel if I have to; but I'm sure that come tomorrow morning he'll be pissed off with me.

I remain silent; I wait without saying anything; I find no judicious words to utter. The uncertainty persists for a minute or so, then the crisis passes. In a strangely feeble, almost trembling voice he says to me: 'We'd best go back. Have to begin first thing in the morning.'

Right, back it is. We'll finish our drinks and back it is. I light a last cigarette, look at Tisserand once more. He really is totally haggard. Wordlessly he lets me pay the bill, wordlessly he follows me as I make for the door. He's stooped, huddled; he's ashamed of himself, hates himself, wishes he were dead.

We walk in the direction of the hotel. In the street it's starting to rain. So there it is, our first day in Rouen over. And I know that on this evidence the days ahead will be absolutely identical.

2

Every Day's a New Day

Witnessed the death of a guy, today, in the Nouvelles Galeries. A very simple death, à la Patricia Highsmith (what I mean is, with that simplicity and brutality characteristic of real life which is also found in the novels of Patricia Highsmith).

Here's how it happened. On entering the part of the store that's arranged as a self-service I observed a man whose face I couldn't see stretched out on the floor (but I subsequently learnt, while listening in on a conversation between the checkout girls, that he must have been about forty). A lot of people were already fussing over him. I went by trying not to linger too long, so as not to show morbid curiosity. It was around six o'clock.

I bought one or two things: cheese and sliced bread to eat in my hotel room (I'd decided to avoid Tisserand's company that particular evening, to relax a bit). But I hesitated a while over the very varied bottles of wine offered up to the covetousness of the public. The problem was I didn't have a corkscrew. And anyway, I don't like wine; this last argument clinched it and I opted for a six-pack of Tuborg.

On arriving at the checkout I learnt from a conversation between the checkout girls and a couple who'd assisted in the life-saving operation, at least in its final phase, that the man was dead. The female partner in the couple was a nurse. She was saying that he should have been given heart massage, that maybe this would have saved him. I don't know, I know nothing about it, but if that was the case then why didn't she do it? I find it hard to comprehend this kind of attitude.

In any event, the conclusion I draw from it all is that in certain circumstances you can so easily depart this life – or not, as the case may be.

It can't be said that this had been a very dignified death, what with all the people passing by pushing their trolleys (it was the busiest time of the day), in that circus atmosphere which always characterizes supermarkets. I remember there was even the Nouvelles Galeries advertising jingle (perhaps they've changed it since); the refrain, in particular, consisted of the following words: *Nouvelles Galeries, todayeee . . . Every day's a new day . . .*

When I came out the man was still there. The body had been wrapped in some carpets, or more likely thick blankets, tied up very tight with string. It was no longer a man but a parcel, heavy and inert, and arrangements were being made for its transport.

All in a day's work. It was six-twenty.

3

The Old Marketplace Game

I know it's crazy but I've decided to stay in Rouen this weekend. Tisserand was astonished to hear it; I explained to him I wanted to see the town and that I had nothing better to do in Paris. I don't really want to see the town.

And yet there are very fine medieval remains, some ancient houses of great charm. Five or six centuries ago Rouen must have been one of the most beautiful towns in France; but now it's ruined. Everything is dirty, grimy, run down, spoiled by the abiding presence of cars, noise, pollution. I don't know who the mayor is, but it only takes ten minutes of walking the streets of the old town to realize that he is totally incompetent, or corrupt.

To make matters worse there are dozens of yobs who roar down the streets on their motorbikes or scooters, and without silencers. They come in from the Rouen suburbs, which are nearing total industrial collapse. Their objective is to make a deafening racket, as disagreeable as possible, a racket which should be unbearable for the local residents. They are completely successful.

I leave my hotel around two. Without thinking, I go in the direction of the Place du Vieux Marché. It is a truly vast square, bordered entirely by cafés, restaurants and luxury shops. It's here that Joan of Arc was burnt more than five hundred years ago. To commemorate the event they've piled up a load of weirdly curved concrete slabs, half stuck in the ground, which turn out on closer inspection to be a church. There are also embryonic lawns, flowerbeds, and some ramps which seem destined for lovers of skateboarding – unless it be for the cars of the disabled, it's hard to tell. But the complexity of the place doesn't end here: there are also shops in the middle of the square, under a sort of concrete rotunda, as well as an edifice which looks like a bus station.

I settle myself on one of the concrete slabs, determined to get to the bottom of things. It seems highly likely that this square is the heart, the central nucleus of the town. Just what game is being played here exactly?

I observe right away that people generally go around in bands, or in little groups of between two and six individuals. No one group is exactly the same as another, it appears to me. Obviously they resemble each other, they resemble each other enormously, but this resemblance could not be called being the same. It's as if they'd elected to embody the antagonism which necessarily goes with any kind of individuation by adopting slightly different behaviour patterns, ways of moving around, formulas for regrouping.

Next I notice that all these people seem satisfied with themselves and the world; it's astonishing, even a little frightening. They quietly saunter around, this one displaying a quizzical smile, that one a moronic look. Some of the youngsters are dressed in leather jackets with slogans borrowed from the more primitive kind of hard rock; you can read phrases on their backs like *Kill them all!* or *Fuck and destroy!*; but all commune in the certainty of passing an agreeable afternoon devoted primarily to consumerism, and thus to contributing to the consolidation of their being.

I observe, lastly, that I feel different from them, without however being able to define the nature of this difference.

I end up tiring of all this pointless people-watching and take refuge in a café. Another mistake. Between the tables there circulates an enormous Alsatian, even more monstrous than most of its race. It stops in front of each customer, as if making up its mind if it should or shouldn't permit itself to bite him.

Six feet away a young girl is seated before a big cup of frothy chocolate. The animal stops for a while in front of her, it sniffs the cup with its snout as if it were going to suddenly lap up the contents with one lick of its tongue. I sense that she's beginning to be afraid. I get up. I want to intervene, I hate such beasts. But finally the dog departs.

After that I drifted through the narrow streets. Completely by chance I went into the Aître Saint-Maclou: a huge and magnificent square courtyard entirely bordered with Gothic sculptures in dark wood.

A bit further on I saw a wedding procession coming out of the church. A truly old-style affair; blue-grey suit, white dress and orange blossom, little bridesmaids . . . I was sitting on a bench not too far from the church steps.

The bride and groom were getting on a bit. A stocky, rather red-faced man who had the look of a rich peasant; a woman a bit larger than him, with a bony face and glasses. I must say, alas, that the whole thing had something ridiculous about it. Some young people passing by were taking the piss out of the newly-weds. Quite.

For a few minutes I was able to observe all this in a strictly objective manner. And then an unpleasant sensation started to come over me. I got to my feet and quickly left.

Two hours later, night having fallen, I came out of my hotel once again. I ate a pizza, standing up, alone, in an establishment that was deserted – and which deserved to remain so. The pizza pastry was revolting. The decor was made up of squares of white mosaic and wall lamps in brushed steel – you'd have thought yourself in an operating theatre.

Then I went to see a porno movie in the one Rouen cinema specializing in such things. The place was half full, which is pretty good these days. Mainly pensioners and immigrants, of course; there were, however, a few couples.

After a while I was surprised to see that people were often changing seats, and for no apparent reason. Wanting to know the rationale for such behaviour I too changed places, at the same time as another guy. In fact it's very simple: each time a couple arrives they find themselves surrounded by two or three men, who install themselves a few seats away and immediately start to masturbate. Their great wish, I think, is that the woman of the couple cast a glance at their dicks.

I stayed in the cinema for around an hour, then recrossed Rouen to go to the station. A few vaguely menacing beggars were hanging about in the concourse. I didn't take any notice of this and jotted down the train times for Paris.

The next morning I got up early, I arrived in good time for the first train; I bought a ticket, waited, and didn't get on it; and I can't for the life of me think why. It's all very unpleasant.

4

It was the following evening that I took ill. After dinner Tisserand wanted to go to a club; I declined the invitation. My left shoulder was hurting me and I was shivering all over. Returning to the hotel, I tried to sleep but it was no good; once out flat I was unable to breathe. I sat up again; the wallpaper was discouraging.

An hour later I started having difficulty breathing, even sitting up. I made it over to the sink. My colour was cadaverous; the pain had begun its slow descent from the shoulder towards the heart. That's when I said to myself that maybe my condition was serious; I'd clearly overdone the cigarettes of late.

I remained leaning against the sink for some twenty minutes, registering the steady increase of the pain. It vexed me greatly to go out again, to go to the hospital, all that.

Around one in the morning I banged the door shut and went out. By now the pain was clearly localized in the heart region. Each breath cost me an enormous effort, and manifested itself as a muffled wheezing. I was scarcely able to walk, except by taking tiny steps, thirty centimetres at very most. I was constantly obliged to lean against the cars.

I rested for a few minutes against a Peugeot 205, then began the ascent of a street that appeared to lead to a more important crossroads. It took me around half an hour to cover five hundred metres. The pain had stopped getting worse, yet went on being intense. On the other hand my difficulty in breathing was becoming more and more serious, and that was most alarming. I had the feeling that if this continued I was going to die within the next few hours, before dawn at any rate. The injustice of such a sudden death hit me; it could hardly be said that I'd abused life. For a few years I was, it's true, in a bit of a bad way; but that was no reason to *interrupt the experiment*; on the contrary it could be maintained, rightly so, that life was contriving to smile on me. In truth, it was all rather badly organized.

What's more, this town and its inhabitants had been instantly repugnant to me. Not only did I not want to die, but above all I did not want to die in Rouen. To die in Rouen, in the midst of the Rouennais, was especially odious to me, even. That would be, I was telling myself in a state of slight delirium probably engendered by the pain, to accord them too great an honour, these idiot Rouennais. I recall this young couple, I'd managed to flag down their car at a red light; they must have come out of a club, at least this is the impression they gave. I ask the way to the hospital; somewhat annoyed, the girl cursorily points it out to me. A moment of silence. I am barely able to speak, barely able to stand, it's obvious I'm in no fit state to get there on my own. I look at them, I wordlessly implore their pity, wondering in the meantime if they actually realize what it is they're doing. And then the lights change to green, and the guy drives off.

Did they exchange a word afterwards to justify their behaviour? There's no certainty they did.

Finally I spot an unhoped-for taxi. I try and seem blasé when announcing that I want to go to the hospital, but it doesn't really work, and the driver comes close to refusing. This pathetic creep will have the gall to say to me, just before moving off, that he 'hopes I won't muck up his seat covers.' As a matter of fact I'd already heard it said that pregnant women face the same problem when going into labour: aside from a few Cambodians all the taxis refuse to take them for fear of finding themselves lumbered with bodily discharges on their back seat.

So let's be off!

Once in the hospital, it has to be said, the formalities are very quick. An intern looks after me, makes me do a whole series of tests. He wishes, I think, to assure himself that I'm not going to die on him within the next hour.

Once the examination is over he comes over to me and announces that I have a pericardial, and not an infarction as he'd first thought. He informs me that the early symptoms are exactly the same; but contrary to the infarction, which is often fatal, the pericardial is a completely benign complaint, it's not the kind of thing you die of. 'You must have been scared,' he says. So as not to complicate things I reply that yes, but in fact I wasn't in the least bit scared. I just had the feeling I was about to snuff it at any moment; that's different.

Next I'm wheeled into the emergency ward. Once sitting on the bed I start sobbing. That helps a little. I'm alone in the ward, I don't have to worry. Every once in a while a nurse pokes her head round the door, assures herself that my sobbing remains more or less constant, and goes away again.

Dawn breaks. A drunk is conveyed to the bed next to mine. I continue sobbing softly, regularly.

Around eight a doctor arrives. He informs me that I'm going to be transferred to the cardiology ward and that he's going to give me an injection to calm me down. They might have thought of this a little sooner, I say to myself. Sure enough the injection sends me straight off to sleep.

On waking up, Tisserand is at my bedside. He has a distracted air, yet is glad to see me at the same time; I'm rather moved by his solicitude. He panicked on not finding me in my room, he has telephoned all over the place: to the departmental headquarters for Agriculture, the police station, our company in Paris . . . He still seems rather worried; what with my white face and my perspiring I can't have a very healthy appearance, that's for sure. I explain to him what a pericardial is, that it's nothing at all, I'll be back to rights in less than two weeks. He wants to have the diagnosis confirmed by a nurse, who knows nothing about it; he demands to see a doctor, the top man, whoever . . . Finally the intern on duty will give him the necessary assurances.

He comes back over to me. He promises to do the training on his own, to phone the company to tell them, to take care of everything; he asks me if I need anything. No, not for the moment. Then he leaves, with a friendly and encouraging grin on his face. I go back to sleep almost straightaway.

5

'These children belong to me, these riches belong to me.'
Thus says the foolish man, and he is full of woe. Truly, one
does not belong to oneself. Wherefore the children? Where-
fore the riches?

— Dhammapada

One soon gets used to hospital. For a whole week I have
been quite seriously ill, I haven't wanted to move or to
speak; but I was seeing people around me who were
chatting, who were speaking to each other of their ill-
nesses with that febrile interest, that delectation which
appears somewhat improper to those in good health; I
was also seeing their families coming to visit. Well,
nobody was complaining, anyway; all had an air of being
rather satisfied with their lot, despite the scarcely natural
way of life being forced on them; despite, too, the
danger hanging over them; because at the end of the day
the life of most of the patients on a cardiology ward is at
risk.

I remember this fifty-five-year-old worker, it was his
sixth stay: he greeted everyone, the doctor, the
nurses . . . He was visibly delighted to be there. And yet
here was a man who in private led an extremely active
life: he was fixing up his house, doing his garden, etc. I

saw his wife, she seemed very nice; they were rather touching in their way, loving each other like that at fifty-odd. But the moment he arrived in hospital he abdicated all responsibility; he happily placed his body in the hands of science. From then on everything was arranged. Some day or other he'd be staying for keeps in this hospital, that much was clear; but that too was arranged. I can see him now, addressing the doctor with a kind of gluttonous impatience, dropping in the odd familiar abbreviation which I didn't understand: 'You're gonna do my pneumo and my venous cath then?' Oh yes, he swore by his venous cath; he talked about it every single day.

By comparison I was conscious of being a rather difficult patient. In point of fact I was experiencing some difficulty getting a grip on myself once again. It's an odd experience seeing one's legs as separate objects, a long way off from one's mind, to which they would be reunited more or less by chance, and badly at that. To imagine oneself, incredulously, as a heap of twitching limbs. And one has need of them, these limbs, one has terrible need of them. All the same they seemed truly bizarre at times, truly strange. Above all the legs.

Tisserand has been to see me twice, he has been wonderful, he has brought me books and pastries. He really wanted to cheer me up, I knew; so I listed some books for him. But I didn't actually fancy reading. My mind was drifting, hazy, somewhat perplexed.

He has made a few erotic wisecracks about the nurses, but that was inevitable, quite natural, and I'm not miffed with him about it. Plus it's a fact that, what with the room temperatures, the nurses are usually half naked beneath their uniforms; just a bra and pants, easily visible through their light clothing. This undeniably maintains a slight but constant erotic tension, all the more so since they are touching you, one is oneself almost naked, etc. And the sick body still wants for sensual pleasure, alas. If the truth be told, I cite this *from memory*; I was myself in a state of almost total erotic insensitivity, at least during the first week.

I really got the feeling the nurses and the other patients were surprised I didn't receive more visits; so I've explained, for their general edification, that I was on a professional visit to Rouen at the moment it all happened; this wasn't my home town, I didn't know a soul. In short, I was there by chance.

Yet wasn't there anybody I wanted to get in touch with, inform about my state? In fact no, there was nobody.

The second week was altogether tougher; I was starting to get better, to manifest the desire to leave. Life was looking up again, as they say. Tisserand was no longer around to bring me pastries; he must have been going through his act for the good people of Dijon.

Listening by chance to the radio Monday morning, I learned that the students had ended their demonstrations, and had of course obtained everything they were asking for. On the other hand an SNCF strike had been called, and had begun in a really tough atmosphere; the trade union officials appeared overwhelmed by the intransigence and violence of the striking railwaymen. Things were proceeding as normal then. The struggle was continuing.

The next morning someone telephoned from my

company, asking to speak to me; an executive secretary had been given this difficult mission. She has been perfect, saying all the right things and assuring me that the reestablishment of my health mattered more to them than anything else. She was nevertheless wishing to know if I would be well enough to go to La Roche-sur-Yon, as planned. I replied that I knew nothing for sure, but that this was my most ardent wish. She laughed, somewhat stupidly; but then she's a very stupid young woman, as I'd already remarked.

6

Rouen–Paris

I left the hospital two days later, rather sooner, I believe, than the doctors would really have wished. Usually they try and keep you in for the longest possible time so as to increase their coefficient of occupied beds; but the holiday period has doubtless inclined them towards clemency. Besides, the head doctor had promised me, 'You'll be home for Christmas': those had been his very words. Home, I don't know; but somewhere, that's for sure.

I made my farewells to the worker, who'd been operated on that same morning. Everything had gone very well, according to the doctors; be that as it may, he had the look of a man whose time was running out.

His wife absolutely insisted I taste the apple tart her husband didn't have the strength to swallow. I accepted; it was delicious.

'Keep your chin up, my son!' he said to me at the moment of leavetaking. I wished him the same. He was right; it's something that can always come in useful, keeping your chin up.

Rouen–Paris. Exactly three weeks before I was making

this same journey in the opposite direction. What's changed in the meantime? Small clusters of houses are still smoking down in the valley, with their promise of peace and tranquillity. The grass is green. There's sunshine, with small clouds forming a contrast; the light is more that of spring. But a bit further away the land is flooded; a slight rippling of the water can be made out between the willows; one imagines a sticky, blackish mud into which the feet suddenly sink.

Not far off from me in the carriage a black guy listens to his Walkman while polishing off a bottle of J&B. He struts down the aisle, bottle in hand. An animal, probably dangerous. I try and avoid his gaze, which is, however, relatively friendly.

An executive type, doubtless disturbed by the black man, comes and plonks himself down opposite me. What's he doing here! He should be in first class. You never get any peace.

He has a Rolex watch, a seersucker jacket. On the third finger of his left hand he wears a conventionally narrow gold wedding ring. His face is squarish, frank, rather likeable. He might be around forty. His pale cream shirt has slightly darker raised pinstripes. His tie is of average width, and of course he's reading *Les Échos*. Not only is he reading them but he's devouring them, as if the meaning of his life might suddenly depend on this reading.

So as not to see him I'm obliged to turn towards the landscape. It's odd, now it seems to me the sun has turned to red, as it was during my trip out. But I don't give much of a damn; there could be five or six red suns out there and it wouldn't make a jot of difference to the course of my meditations.

I don't like this world. I definitely do not like it. The society in which I live disgusts me; advertising sickens me; computers make me puke. My entire work as a computer expert consists of adding to the data, the cross-referencing, the criteria of rational decision-making. It has no meaning. To tell the truth, it is even negative up to a point; a useless encumbering of the neurons. This world has need of many things, bar more information.

The arrival in Paris, as grim as ever. The leprous façades of the Pont Cardinet flats, behind which one invariably imagines retired folk agonizing alongside their cat Poucette which is eating up half their pension with its Friskies. Those weird metal structures that indecently mount each other to form a grid of overhead wires. And the inevitable advertising hoardings flashing by, gaudy and repellent. 'A gay and changing spectacle on the walls.' Bullshit. Pure fucking bullshit.

7

I got back to my apartment without real enthusiasm; the post consisted of a payment reminder for an erotic phone line (*Natacha, with the hots for you*) and a long letter from the Trois Suisses informing me of the setting up of a telecomputer service for simplified ordering, the Chouchoutel. In my capacity as a special client I could profit from this right away; the entire computer team (inset photos) had worked flat out so that the service would be operative by Christmas; the commercial directrice of the Trois Suisses was pleased to be in the position to personally assign me a Chouchou code.

The call-counter of my answer machine registered the figure 1, which surprised me a bit; must be a wrong number. In response to my message a weary and contemptuous female voice had come out with 'You pathetic creep' before hanging up. In short, there was nothing keeping me in Paris.

In any case I really fancied going to the Vendée. The Vendée brought back lots of holiday memories for me (rather bad ones in fact, but such is life). I'd retraced some of these in the form of an animal story called *Dialogues Between a Dachshund and a Poodle*, which could be deemed an adolescent self-portrait. In the final chapter of this work one of the dogs is reading aloud, to his companion, a manuscript found in the roll-top desk of his young master:

'Last year, around 23 August, I was walking along the beach at Les Sables d'Olonne, accompanied by my poodle. Whereas my four-legged friend seemed to unconstrainedly enjoy the motions of the sea air and the brightness of the sun (particularly keen and delightful on this late morning), I was unable to prevent the vice of reflection from squeezing my translucid brow, and, crushed by the weight of a too-heavy burden, my head was sinking sadly on my breast.

'On this occasion I stopped before a young girl who may have been fourteen or so. She was playing badminton with her father, or some other game that is played with rackets and a shuttlecock. Her clothing bore evidence of the most candid simplicity, given that she was in a bathing costume, and with naked breasts to boot. Nevertheless, and at this stage one can only bow before such perseverance, her whole attitude manifested the deployment of an ongoing attempt at seduction. The ascending movement of her arms at the moment she missed the projectile, although it had the added advantage of pushing forward the two ochraceous globes constituting an already more than nascent bosom, was principally accompanied by a smile at once amused and disconsolate, ultimately replete with an intense joie de vivre, which she was manifestly directing at all the adolescent males passing within a radius of fifty metres. And this, let it be noted, in the very midst of an activity both eminently sportive and familial in character.

'Her little stratagem was not, moreover, without producing its effect, as I was quick to realize; drawing near to her, the boys were rolling their shoulders, and the cadenced scissoring of their gait was slowing to a noteworthy degree. Turning her head towards them with a lively movement which provoked in her hair a temporary dishevelment not denuded of a saucy grace, she then bestowed upon the most interesting of her victims a fleeting smile immediately contradicted by a no less charming movement aimed this time at hitting the shuttlecock dead centre.

'And so I found myself returning once again to a subject of meditation which for years has not ceased haunting my thoughts: why, having once attained a certain age, do boys and girls reciprocally pass their time in flirting and seducing each other?

'Certain people will say, in a charming voice, "It is the awakening of sexual desire, no more no less, that is all." I understand this point of view; I have myself long shared it. It can pride itself in mobilizing on its side the multiple lineaments of thought which intersect, as translucid jelly, at our ideological horizon as well as in the robust centripetal force of good sense. It might, then, seem audacious, even suicidal, to run smack into its incontrovertible premises. This I shall not do. I am very far, in fact, from seeking to deny the existence and the strength of sexual desire in adolescent humans. Tortoises themselves feel it and do not venture, in these troubled times, to importune their young master. It nonetheless remains a fact that certain grave and concordant indices, like a rosary of strange facts, have progressively led me to suppose the existence of a more profound and more hidden force, a veritable existential nodosity from whence desire would arise. I have not, hitherto, personally informed anyone of this, so as not to dissipate in idle chatter the credit for mental health that men have generally accorded me during the time of our relations. But my conviction has now taken shape, and it is time to speak out.

'Example number 1. Let us consider a group of young people who are together of an evening, or indeed on holiday in Bulgaria. Among these young people there exists a previously formed couple; let us call the boy François and the girl Françoise. We will have before us a concrete, banal and easily observable example.

'Let us abandon these young people to their amusing activities, but before that let us clip from their actual experience a number of aleatory temporal segments which we will film with the aid of a high-speed camera concealed in the environs. It is apparent from a series of measurements that Françoise and François will spend around 37% of their time in kissing and canoodling, in short in bestowing marks of the greatest reciprocal tenderness.

'Let us now repeat the experiment in annulling the aforesaid social environment, which is to say that Françoise and François will be alone. The percentage drops straightaway to 17%.

'Example number 2. I wish to speak to you now of a poor young girl whose name was Brigitte Bardot. Yes, it's true. In my sixth-form class there really was a girl called Bardot, since her father was called thus. I have looked up various information on him: he was a scrap merchant from near Trilport. His wife was not working;

she stayed at home. These people hardly ever went to the cinema, I am persuaded they didn't call her by this name deliberately; perhaps for the first few years they were even amused by the coincidence . . . It is difficult to say.

'At the time I knew her, in the bloom of her seventeen years, Brigitte Bardot was truly repulsive. First of all she was extremely fat, a porker and even a super-porker, with abundant rolls of fat gracelessly disposed at the intersections of her obese body. Yet had she followed a slimming diet of the most frightening severity for twenty-five years her fate would not have been markedly improved. Because her skin was blotchy, puffy and acned. And her face was wide, flat and round, with little deep-set eyes, and straggly, lustreless hair. Indeed, the comparison with a sow forced itself on everyone in an inevitable and natural way.

'She had no girlfriends, and obviously no boyfriends. She was therefore completely alone. Nobody addressed a word to her, not even during a physics test; they would always prefer to address themselves to someone else. She came to classes then returned home; never did I hear it said that someone might have seen her other than at school.

'During classes certain people sat next to her; they got used to her massive presence. They didn't notice her and neither did they poke fun at her. She didn't participate in discussions in the philosophy class; she didn't participate in anything at all. She wouldn't have been more tranquil on the planet Mars.

'I suppose her parents must have loved her. What would she do of an evening, after getting home?

Because she surely must have had a room, with a bed, and some teddies dating from her childhood. She must have watched the telly with her parents. A dark room, and three beings united by the photonic flux; such is the image I have.

'As for Sundays, I can well imagine the immediate family welcoming her with feigned cordiality. And her cousins, probably pretty. A depressing thought.

'Did she have fantasies, and if so which? Romantic ones à la Barbara Cartland? I find it hard to believe that she might have somehow imagined, be it only in dream, that a young man of good family pursuing his studies in medicine would one day nourish the prospect of taking her in his open-top car to visit the abbeys of the Normandy coast. Unless, perhaps, she were previously provided with a penitent's hood, so lending a mysterious edge to the adventure.

'Her hormonal mechanisms must have functioned normally, there's no reason to suppose otherwise. And then? Does that suffice for having erotic fantasies? Did she imagine masculine hands lingering between the folds of her obese belly? Descending as far as her sexual parts? I turn to medicine and medicine can afford me no answer. There are many things concerning Bardot I have not managed to elucidate. I have tried.

'I didn't go as far as sleeping with her. I merely took the first steps along the path which normally leads to this. To be exact, I began at the beginning of November to speak to her, a few words at the end of class, nothing more than this for a whole fortnight. And then, on two or three occasions I asked her for explanations on such and such a point of mathematics; all this with great prudence, and without drawing attention to myself. Around mid-December I began to touch her hand, in a seemingly accidental way. Each time she reacted as if to an electric shock. It was rather impressive.

'The culminating point of our relations was attained just before Christmas, when I again accompanied her to her train (in reality a rail-car). As the station was more than eight hundred metres away this was no mean feat; I was even spotted on this occasion. In class I was generally taken to be a rather weird person, so this in fact only did limited harm to my social image.

'That evening, in the middle of the platform, I kissed her on the cheek. I did not kiss her on the mouth. What is more I think that paradoxically she would not have permitted this, since even if her lips and her tongue had never ever known the experience of contact with a masculine tongue she nonetheless had a very precise idea of the time and place when this operation ought to take place within the archetypal unfolding of adolescent flirting, I would even say that a more precise idea than the latter had never had occasion to be rectified and assuaged by the fluid vapour of the lived instant.

'Immediately after the Christmas holidays I stopped speaking to her. The guy who had spotted me near the station seemed to have forgotten the incident, but I had been afraid even so. In any case, dating Bardot would have demanded a moral strength far superior to the one I could, even at the time, pride myself on. Because not only was she ugly but she was plain nasty. Goaded on by sexual liberation (it was right at the beginning of the 80s, AIDS still did not exist), she couldn't make appeal to some ethical notion of virginity, obviously. On top of that she was too intelligent and too lucid to account for her state as being a product of "Judeo-Christian influence" – in any case her parents were agnostics. All means of evasion were thus closed to her. She could only assist, in silent hatred, at the liberation of others; witness the boys pressing themselves like crabs against others' bodies; sense the relationships being formed, the experiments being undertaken, the orgasms surging forth; live to the full a silent self-destruction when faced with the flaunted pleasure of others. Thus was her adolescence to unfold, and thus it unfolded: jealousy and frustration fermented slowly to become a swelling of paroxystic hatred.

'In the end I am not terribly proud of this story. The whole thing was too manifestly ludicrous to be devoid of cruelty. For example I recall myself greeting her one morning with these words, "Oh, you have a new dress, Brigitte." It was really repulsive, even if true; because the fact is amazing but nonetheless real: *she'd changed her dress*, I even remember one time when she'd put *a ribbon in her hair*: Oh my God! a calf's head decorated with chopped parsley, more like. I implore her pardon in the name of all humanity.

'The desire for love is deep in man, it plunges its roots to astonishing depths, and the multiplicity of its radicles is intercalated in the very substance of the heart. Despite the avalanche of humiliations which made up her daily life, Brigitte Bardot waited and hoped. She is probably waiting and hoping still. In her situation a viper would already have committed suicide. Mankind is supremely self-confident.

★

'After having taken a long and hard look at the echelon-
ment of the various appendices of the sexual function,
the moment appears to have arrived to expound the
central theorem of my apocritique. Unless you were to
put a halt to the implacable unfolding of my reasoning
with the objection that, good prince, I will permit you
to formulate: "You take all your examples from adolescence, which is indeed an important period in life,
but when all is said and done it only occupies an exceedingly brief fraction of this. Are you not afraid, then, that
your conclusions, the finesse and rigour of which we
admire, may ultimately turn out to be both partial and
limited?" To this amiable adversary I will reply that adolescence is not only an important period in life, but that
it is the only period where one may speak of life in the
full sense of the word. The attractile drives are unleashed
around the age of thirteen, after which they gradually
diminish, or rather they are resolved in models of
behaviour which are, after all, only constrained forces.
The violence of the initial explosion means that the
outcome of the conflict may remain uncertain for years;
this is what is called a transitory regime in electrody-
namics. But little by little the oscillations become slower,
to the point of resolving themselves in mild and melan-
cholic long waves; from this moment on all is decided,
and life is nothing more than a preparation for death.
This can be expressed in a more brutal and less exact
way by saying that man is a diminished adolescent.

'After having taken a long and hard look at the ech-
elonment of the various appendices of the sexual
function, the moment seems to me to have come to
expound the central theorem of my apocritique. For

this I will utilize the lever of a condensed but adequate formulation, to wit:

Sexuality is a system of social hierarchy

'At this stage it will more than ever behove me to swathe my formulation in the austere garb of rigour. The ideological enemy is often crouching close to the target, and with a long cry of hatred he throws himself, at the entry to the last bend, on the imprudent thinker who, intoxicated from feeling the first rays of truth already alighting on his anaemic brow, had stupidly neglected to guard his rear. I will not imitate this error, and, letting the candelabra of stupefaction light themselves in your brains, I will continue to unwind the coils of my reasoning with the silent moderation of the rattlesnake. Thus I will take care to ignore the objection any attentive reader would not fail to confront me with: in the second example I surreptitiously introduced the concept of love, whereas until now my argument was based on pure sexuality. Contradiction? Incoherence? Ha ha ha!

'The marriage of Marthe and Martin goes back forty-three years. As they were married at twenty-one this makes them sixty-four. They are already retired or close to being so, in accordance with the social regulations which apply in their case. They will, as they say, end their lives together. In these circumstances it is patently obvious that the entity "couple" is formed, pertinent outside of any social contract, and which even manages on certain minor levels to equal or exceed in importance the old ape that is man. In my opinion it is within this framework that the possibility of giving a meaning to the word "love" can be reconsidered.

'After having girded my thought with the sharpened stakes of restriction I can now add that, despite its onto-logical fragility, the concept of love possesses or used to possess until recently all the attributes of a prodigious operative energy. Forged in haste, it quickly met with a large audience, and rare are those who clearly and deliberately renounce loving, even in our own times. This transparent success would tend to demonstrate a mysterious correspondence with some unknown con-stituent need of human nature. However, and it is precisely on this point that the aware analyst parts company with the spinner of idle tales, I shall be careful not to formulate the most succinct hypothesis on the nature of the aforesaid need. *Be that as it may, love exists, since one can observe its effects*. Here is a phrase worthy of Claude Bernard, and I want to dedicate it to him. O unassailable savant! it is no mere accident that the obser-vations most distant in appearance from the object that you initially considered come to be lined up one after the other, like so many plump partridges, beneath the radiant majesty of your protective halo. It must indeed possess a very great power, the experimental protocol you set out in 1865 with such rare penetration, for the most extravagant facts to only manage to cross the tenebrous frontier of scientificity after having been situ-ated within the rigidity of your inflexible laws. I salute you, unforgettable physiologist, and I loudly declare that I shall do nothing which might, however minimally, curtail the length of your reign.

'Clearly setting down the columns of an indubitable

axiomatic, I will thirdly cause it to be observed that, contrary to appearances, the vagina is much more than a hole in a lump of meat. (Yes, I know that butcher boys masturbate using escalopes . . . Long may they do so! It is not this which will hold back the prosecution of my thought!) In reality the vagina serves or used to serve until quite recently for the reproduction of the species. Yes, the species.

'Certain writers of the past have thought fit, in evoking the vagina and its attendant parts, to sport the stupidly dumb expression and blank look of a milestone. On the contrary, various others, akin to saprophytes, have wallowed in baseness and cynicism. Like the experienced pilot I shall navigate at equal distance from these symmetrical reefs; better still, I shall rely upon the trajectory of their mid-perpendicular to open my ample and intransigent passage towards the idyllic regions of precise reasoning. The three noble truths that have just lit up your eyes must therefore be considered as the generating trihedron of a pyramid of wisdom which, unprecedented marvel, will fly light-winged over the weathered oceans of doubt. It is sufficient to underline their importance. Notwithstanding that at the present time they somewhat suggest, in their size and their abrupt character, three columns of granite erected in the middle of the desert (such as can be observed, for example, in the plain of Thebes). It would, on the whole, be inimical and hardly consistent with the spirit of this treatise if I were to abandon my reader facing their overbearing verticality. It is for this that the joyous spirals of diverse adventitious propositions will seek to entwine themselves about these first axioms, propositions that I am now going to outline . . .'

Naturally, the work was unfinished. Furthermore, the dachshund dropped off to sleep before the end of the poodle's speech; yet certain indices would lead one to assume that it was in possession of the truth, and that the latter could be expressed in a few sober phrases. In the end I was young, I was having fun. It was before Véronique, all that; they were the good times. I remember at the age of seventeen, when I was once expressing contradictory and confused thoughts on the world, a fifty-year-old woman encountered in a buffet car had said to me, 'You'll see, as you get older things get much simpler.' How right she was!

8

Back to the Cows

At 5.52 on a bitterly cold morning the train made its way into La Roche-sur-Yon. The town was silent, peaceful; absolutely peaceful. 'Right, then!' I say to myself. 'Now's the time for a little walk in the countryside . . .'

I passed through the deserted, or practically deserted, streets of the suburbs. At first I tried comparing the characteristics of the semis but it was really difficult, the sun not having come up yet; I quickly gave it up.

A few of the inhabitants were already up and about, despite the early hour; they watched me go by from their garages. They seemed to be asking themselves what I was doing there. If they'd have questioned me I'd have been hard pressed to give them an answer. In fact nothing justified my presence here. Neither here nor anywhere else, to tell the truth.

Then I arrived in the countryside proper. There were fences, and behind the fences cows. A slight blueness announced the approach of dawn.

I looked at the cows. Most of them weren't asleep, they'd already started grazing. I remarked to myself that they were right; they must have been cold, may as well take a little exercise. I observed them benevolently, without in the least intending to disturb their early-morning peace and quiet. Some of them came over to the fence, without mooing, and looked at me. They were leaving me in peace too. That was fine.

Later I took myself off to the departmental head-quarters for Agriculture. Tisserand was already there; he shook my hand with surprising warmth.

The director was waiting for us in his office. He turned out, right away, to be a rather likeable guy; obvi-ously a kind and simple soul. On the other hand he was totally impervious to the technological message we were supposed to bring him. Computers, he tells us bluntly, he wants nothing to do with them. He has no wish to change his work habits just for the sake of being modern. Things are going nicely the way they are, and they'll go on doing so at least as long as he's here. If he's agreed to our coming it's only for not having hassles with the Ministry, but the moment we've gone he'll put the software in a cupboard and not touch it again.

In these circumstances the training sessions appeared to be an amiable pleasantry, a way of chatting to pass the time. That didn't bother me in the least.

Over the next few days I realize that Tisserand is gradually losing it. After Christmas he leaves to go skiing with an Under-25s club; the 'no boring old farts' kind, with evenings in the discothèque and breakfasting late; in short, the kind where you do a lot of fucking. But he evokes the prospect without enthusiasm; I get the feeling he doesn't believe it for a minute. From time to time his bespectacled gaze drifts aimlessly over me. He gives the impression of being bewitched. I know how it is; I experienced the same thing two years ago, just after my separation from Véronique. You get the feeling you can roll about on the ground, slash your veins with a razor blade or masturbate in the métro and nobody will pay any attention, nobody will lift a finger. As if you were protected from the world by a transparent film, inviolable and perfect. Anyway Tisserand said so the other day (he'd been drinking): 'I feel like a shrink-wrapped chicken leg on a supermarket shelf.' He's also come out with: 'I feel like a frog in formaldehyde. Besides, I resemble a frog, don't I?' I gently replied 'Raphaël . . .' in a reproachful tone. He started; it's the first time I've called him by his Christian name. He was flustered and didn't say a word.

The next morning at breakfast he stared long and hard at his bowl of Nesquik; and then in an almost dreamy voice he sighed, 'Fuck it! I'm twenty-eight and still a virgin!' I was astonished, even so; he then explained that a vestige of pride had always stopped him from *going with whores*. I upbraided him for this; a bit too strongly perhaps, since he persisted in explaining his point of view to me again that very evening, just before leaving to Paris for the weekend. We were in the parking lot of the departmental head office for Agri-culture; the street lamps were exuding an extremely unpleasant yellowish light; the air was cold and damp. He said, 'I've done my sums, you see; I've enough to pay for one whore a week; Saturday evening, that'd be good. Maybe I'll end up doing it. But I know that some men can get the same thing for free, *and with love to boot*. I prefer trying; for the moment I still prefer trying.'

Obviously, I couldn't come up with anything to say,

but I returned to my hotel deep in thought. It's a fact, I mused to myself, that in societies like ours sex truly represents a second system of differentiation, completely independent of money; and as a system of differentiation it functions just as mercilessly. The effects of these two systems are, furthermore, strictly equivalent. Just like unrestrained economic liberalism, and for similar reasons, sexual liberalism produces phenomena of *absolute pauperization*. Some men make love every day; others five or six times in their life, or never. Some make love with dozens of women; others with none. It's what's known as 'the law of the market'. In an economic system where unfair dismissal is prohibited, every person more or less manages to find their place. In a sexual system where adultery is prohibited, every person more or less manages to find their bed mate. In a totally liberal economic system certain people accumulate considerable fortunes; others stagnate in unemployment and misery. In a totally liberal sexual system certain people have a varied and exciting erotic life; others are reduced to masturbation and solitude. Economic liberalism is an extension of the domain of the struggle, its extension to all ages and all classes of society. Sexual liberalism is likewise an extension of the domain of the struggle, its extension to all ages and all classes of society. On the economic plane Raphaël Tisserand belongs in the victors' camp; on the sexual plane in that of the vanquished. Certain people win on both levels; others lose on both. Businesses fight over certain young professionals; women fight over certain young men; men fight over certain young women; the trouble and strife are considerable.

★

A little later I came out of my hotel with the clear intention of getting pissed. I found a café open opposite the station; a few teenagers were playing pinball and that was about it. After the third cognac my thoughts turned to Gérard Leverrier.

Gérard Leverrier was an administrator in the Assemblée Nationale, in the same department as Véronique (who was working there as a secretary). Gérard Leverrier was twenty-six and earned thirty thousand francs a month. However, Gérard Leverrier was shy and prone to depression. One Friday evening in December (he didn't have to go back on the Monday; somewhat against his better judgment he'd taken a fortnight off 'for the holidays'), Gérard Leverrier went back home and put a bullet in his brains.

The news of his death didn't really surprise anyone in the Assemblée Nationale; he was mainly known there for the problems he was encountering in buying himself a bed. He'd decided on the purchase months before; but the realization of his project was proving impossible. The tale was usually told with a faint ironic smile; yet there was nothing to laugh about; these days the purchase of a bed does present enormous difficulties, enough to drive you to suicide. To begin with delivery has to be arranged, and then usually half a day taken off work, with all the problems that entails. Sometimes the delivery men don't come, or maybe they don't manage to get the bed up the stairs and you are obliged to ask for another half-day off. These problems recur for all furniture and domestic appliances, and the accumulation of difficulties resulting from this can already be enough to seriously unhinge a sensitive person. Of all your furniture the bed poses a particular, eminently distressing problem. If you want to retain the goodwill of the salesman you are obliged to buy a double bed, whether you need one or not, whether you have the room for it or not. To buy a single bed is to publicly admit you don't have a sex life, and that you don't envisage having one in the near or even distant future (beds last a long time these days, way beyond the guarantee date; it's a matter of five, ten or even twenty years; this is a serious investment, which commits you in practical terms for the rest of your days; beds last on an average much longer than marriages, as is well-known). Even the purchase of a 140-centimetre bed makes you pass for a stingy and narrow petit-bourgeois; in the salesmen's eyes the 160-centimetre bed is the only one really worth buying; in which case you have a right to their respect, to their consideration, even to a slight knowing smile; this they only grant for the 160-centimetre bed.

On the evening of Gérard Leverrier's death his father phoned up his work; since he was out of the office it was Véronique who took the call. The message was simply to phone his father urgently; she forgot to pass it on. So Gérard Leverrier got back home at six without knowing about the message and put a bullet in his brains. Véronique told me this the evening of the day they learnt about his death at the Assemblée Nationale; she added that it 'scared the shit out of her'; those were her exact words. I imagined she was going to feel some sort of guilt, remorse; not at all; she'd already forgotten by the next morning.

Véronique was 'in analysis', as they say; today I regret

ever having met her. Generally speaking, there's nothing to be had from women in analysis. A woman fallen into the hands of the psychoanalysts becomes absolutely unfit for use, as I've discovered time and again. This phenomenon should not be taken as a secondary effect of psychoanalysis, but rather as its principal goal. Under the pretext of reconstructing the ego psychoanalysts proceed, in reality, to a scandalous destruction of the human being. Innocence, generosity, purity . . . all such things are rapidly crushed by their uncouth hands. Handsomely remunerated, pretentious and stupid, psychoanalysts reduce to absolute zero any aptitude in their so-called patients for love, be it mental or physical; in fact they behave as true enemies of mankind. A ruthless school of egoism, psychoanalysis cynically lays into decent, slightly fucked-up young women and transforms them into vile scumbags of such delirious egocentrism as to warrant nothing but well-earned contempt. On no account must any confidence be placed in a woman who's passed through the hands of the psychoanalysts. Pettiness, egoism, arrogant stupidity, complete lack of moral sense, a chronic inability to love: there you have an exhaustive portrait of the 'analysed' woman.

Véronique, it has to be said, corresponded blow by blow to this description. I loved her – to the extent that it was within my power – which represents a lot of love. This love was poured down the drain, I now realize; I'd have done better to break both her arms. Like all depressives she doubtless always had a tendency towards egoism and a lack of feeling; but her psychoanalysis transformed her once and for all into a total shit, lacking both guts and conscience – a detritus wrapped in silver paper. I remember she had a white plastic board on which she ordinarily wrote things like 'petits pois' or 'dry cleaners'. One evening, coming back from her *session*, she'd noted down this phrase of Lacan's: 'the viler you are, the better it will be.' I'd smiled; in this I was wrong. At this stage the phrase was still only a *programme*; but she was going to put it into practice, point by point.

One evening when Véronique was out I swallowed a bottle of Largactyl. Gripped by panic, I called the emergency services straightaway. They had to take me to hospital, give me a stomach pump, etc. In fine, I only just made it. That bastard (what else can you call her?) didn't even come and see me in hospital. On getting back 'home', if it can be called that, all she managed to find as words of welcome was that I was an egoist and a flake; her interpretation of the incident was that I was contriving to cause her extra worry, she 'who already had enough on her plate with problems at work.' The vile bitch even claimed I was indulging in 'emotional blackmail'; when I think of it now, I regret not taking a knife to her ovaries. But then this is all in the past.

I also recall the evening she'd called the cops to get me thrown out of her place. Why 'her place'? Because the apartment was in her name, and she was paying the rent more often than I was. And that's the first effect of psychoanalysis; to develop an unbelievably ridiculous avarice and pettiness in its victims. Waste of time trying to go to the café with someone who's doing analysis: he inevitably starts discussing the fine points of the bill, and that leads to problems with the waiter. In short there were these three idiot cops with their walkie-talkies and their air of knowing more about life than anybody else. I was in pyjamas and shivering from the cold; my hands were gripping the table legs, under the tablecloth; I was absolutely determined to make them take me by force. During all this my scumbag friend was showing them the rent receipts in order to establish her rights to the place; she was probably hoping they'd get their truncheons out. That same evening she'd had a 'session'; her whole stock of meanness and egoism was replenished; but I didn't give in, I asked for a warrant, and those stupid policemen had to quit the premises. Anyway, I left for good the next morning.

9

Buccaneer Cottages

All of a sudden it didn't bother me not being modern.
— Roland Barthes

Early Saturday morning I find a taxi-driver on the Place de la Gare who agrees to drive me to Les Sables-d'Olonne.

On leaving the town we pass through successive banks of mist, then, emerging from the last, we plunge into an absolute sea of dense fog. The road and the landscape are completely inundated. Nothing can be made out, save the odd tree or cow which emerges as a fleeting blur. It is very beautiful.

Arriving by the sea, the weather suddenly clears. There's a wind, a lot of wind, but the sky is almost blue; some clouds are scudding rapidly east. I get out of the taxi after giving the driver a tip, which earns me a 'Have a nice day', uttered somewhat grudgingly it seems to me. He probably thinks I'm going fishing for crabs, something of the sort.

For a while I actually do stroll along the beach. The sea is grey, rather choppy. I don't feel anything much. I walk for a good while.

Around eleven people begin arriving with their kids and dogs. I turn in the opposite direction.

At the end of the beach at Les Sables-d'Olonne, in the prolongation of the jetty that seals off the port, there are a few old houses and a Romanesque church. Nothing overly spectacular: these are edifices of robust coarse stone built to withstand the storms, and which have withstood the storms for hundreds of years. You can readily imagine the ancient way of life of the Sables fishermen, with Sunday mass in the little church, communion for the faithful, while the wind howls outside and the ocean pounds against the rocky coast. It was a life without distraction and without incident, dominated by a tough and dangerous job of work. A simple and rustic life, full of nobility. An extremely stupid way of life, too.

Not far from these houses are some modern white residences meant for holidaymakers. There's a whole bunch of these apartment blocks, of a height varying between ten and twenty floors. The blocks are laid out on a multi-level promenade, the lower level being arranged as a parking lot. I walked for a long time from one block to the other, which permits me to affirm that the bulk of the apartments must, by virtue of various architectural ploys, have a view of the sea. At this time of year everything was deserted, and the whistling of the wind swirling between the concrete structures had something truly sinister about it.

I then made for a more recent and luxurious residence, this time situated just a few metres from the sea. It bore the name 'Buccaneer Cottages'. The ground floor was made up of a supermarket, a pizzeria and a discothèque; all three of them shut. A placard extended an invitation to visit the show flat.

This time an unpleasant sensation began taking hold of me. To imagine a family of holidaymakers returning to their Buccaneer Cottage before going to scoff their escalope of veal in pirate sauce, and that their youngest daughter might go and get laid in a 'Ye Olde Cape-Horner'-style nightspot, was all becoming a bit too much; but there was nothing I could do about it.

By now I was hungry. I hooked up with a dentist at a waffle-seller's stand. In fact 'hooked up' is stretching it a bit; let's just say we exchanged a few words while waiting for the vendor to come back. I don't know why he thought it necessary to inform me that he was a dentist. In general I hate dentists; I take them to be exceedingly venal creatures whose only goal in life is to wrench out the most teeth possible and buy themselves a Mercedes with a sun-roof. And this one didn't have the air of being any exception to the rule.

Somewhat absurdly I thought it necessary to justify my presence one more time and spun him a whole line about how I had the intention of buying an apartment in Buccaneer Cottages. His interest was awakened right away, and with waffle in hand he weighed up the pros and cons for a while before finally concluding that the investment 'seemed wise to him'. I ought to have guessed.

10

The Port of Call

Ah yes, to have values! . . .

When I got back to La Roche-sur-Yon I bought a steak knife in the Unico; I was beginning to perceive the rudiments of a plan.

Sunday was non-existent; Monday particularly dreary. I sensed, without needing to ask him, that Tisserand had had a lousy weekend; this didn't surprise me in the least. It was already 22 December.

The following evening we went to eat in a pizzeria. The waiter had the air of actually being Italian; one imagined him to be both hairy and charming; he deeply disgusted me. On top of that he hurriedly set down our respective spaghettis without due care. Ah, if we'd been wearing slit skirts that would have been different! . . .

Tisserand was knocking back huge glasses of wine; I was evoking different tendencies within contemporary dance music. He wasn't responding; in fact I don't think he was even listening. Nevertheless, when I briefly described the time-honoured alternation of fast and slow records, so as to underline the ritual character it had lent to the procedures of seduction, his interest was re-awakened (had he already had occasion, personally, to dance to a slow number? It was by no means certain). I went on to the offensive:

—I suppose you're doing something for Christmas. With the folks, no doubt . . .

—We do nothing at Christmas, I'm Jewish, he informed me with a touch of pride. At least, my parents are Jewish, he added in an undertone.

This revelation shut me up for a few seconds. But after all, Jewish or not, did that really change anything? If so, I couldn't see what. I pressed on.

—What about doing something on the 24th? I know a club in Les Sables, *The Port of Call*. Very friendly . . .

I had the feeling my words were ringing false; I was ashamed of myself. But Tisserand was no longer in any state to pay attention to such subtleties. 'Do you think there'll be lots of people? I get the impression the 24th is very "family",' that was his feeble, pathetic objection. I conceded that of course the 31st would be much better: 'Girls really like *to sleep around* on the 31st,' I asserted with authority. But for all that the 24th wasn't to be dismissed: 'Girls eat oysters with the parents and the grandmother, receive their presents. But after midnight they go clubbing,' I was getting excited, believing my own story; Tisserand proved easy to convince, just as I'd predicted.

The following evening he took three hours to get ready. I waited for him while playing dominoes in the hotel lounge; I played both hands at once, it was really boring; all the same I was rather anxious.

He showed up dressed in a black suit and a gold tie;

his hair must have taken him a good while; they make gels now that give the most surprising results. In the end a black outfit was what suited him best; poor schmuck.

We still had almost an hour to kill; there was no point in going clubbing before eleven-thirty, I was categorical about that. After a brief discussion we went to have a look-see at the midnight mass; the priest was speaking of an immense hope rising in the hearts of men; I found nothing to object to in that. Tisserand was getting bored, was thinking of other things; I began to feel somewhat disgusted, but I had to go through with it. I'd placed the steak knife in a plastic bag in the front of the car.

I found *The Port of Call* again without difficulty; I'd passed many a dull evening there, it has to be said. This was going back more than ten years; but unpleasant memories are erased less quickly than one thinks.

The club was half-full: mainly of twenty-five-year-olds, which immediately did for the modest chances of Tisserand. A lot of miniskirts, low-cut bustiers; in short, fresh meat. I saw his eyes suddenly pop out on taking in the dance floor; I left to order a bourbon at the bar. On my return he was already standing nervously at the edge of the clutch of dancers. I vaguely murmured 'I'll rejoin you in a minute', and made off towards a table whose slightly prominent position would afford me an excellent view of the theatre of operations.

To begin with Tisserand appeared to be interested in a twenty-something brunette, a secretary most like. I was highly inclined to approve of his choice. On the one hand the girl was no great beauty, and would doubtless be a pushover; her breasts, though good-sized, were already a bit slack, and her buttocks appeared flaccid; in a few years, one felt, all this would sag completely. On the other hand her somewhat audacious get-up unambiguously underlined her intention to find a sexual partner: her thin taffeta dress twirled with every movement, revealing a suspender belt and minuscule g-string in black lace which left her buttocks completely naked. To be sure, her serious, even slightly obstinate face seemed to indicate a prudent character; here was a girl who must surely carry condoms in her bag.

For a few minutes Tisserand danced not far from her, thrusting his arms forward energetically to indicate the enthusiasm the music caused in him. On two or three occasions he even clapped his hands to the beat; but the girl didn't seem to notice him in the least. Profiting from a short break between records he took the initiative and addressed a few words to her. She turned, threw him a scornful glance and took off across the dance floor to get away from him. That was that.

Everything was going as planned. I left to order a second bourbon at the bar.

On my return I sensed that something new was in the offing. A girl was sitting at the table next to mine, alone. She was much younger than Véronique, she might have been seventeen; that aside, she horribly resembled her. Her extremely simple, rather ample dress of beige did not really show off the contours of her body; they scarcely had need of it. The wide hips, the firm and smooth buttocks; the suppleness of the waist which leads the hands up to a pair of round, ample and soft breasts;

the hands which rest confidently on the waist, espousing the noble rotundity of the hips. I knew it all; all I had to do was close my eyes to remember. Up to the face, full and candid, expressing the calm seduction of the natural woman, confident of her beauty. The calm serenity of the young filly, still frisky, eager to try out her limbs in a short gallop. The calm tranquillity of Eve, in love with her own nakedness, knowing herself to be obviously and eternally desirable. I realized that two years of separation had changed nothing; I knocked back my bourbon in one. This was the moment Tisserand chose to return; he was perspiring slightly; he spoke to me; I think he wished to know if I intended trying something with the girl. I didn't reply; I was starting to feel like vomiting, and I had a hard-on; things were at a pretty pass. I said 'Excuse me a moment,' and crossed the discothèque in the direction of the toilets. Once inside I put two fingers down my throat, but the amount of vomit proved feeble and disappointing. Then I masturbated with altogether greater success: I began thinking of Véronique a bit, of course, but then I concentrated on vaginas in general and that did the trick. Ejaculation came after a couple of minutes; it brought me a feeling of confidence and certainty.

On my return I saw that Tisserand had engaged in conversation with the pseudo-Véronique; she was regarding him calmly and without contempt. I knew deep down that this young girl was a marvel; but it was no big deal, I'd done my masturbating. From the amorous point of view Véronique belonged, as we all do, to a *sacrificed generation*. She had certainly been capable of love; she would have wished to still be capable of it, I'll say that for her; but it was no longer possible. A scarce, artificial and belated phenomenon, love can only blossom under certain mental conditions, rarely conjoined, and totally opposed to the freedom of morals which characterizes the modern era. Véronique had known too many discothèques, too many lovers; such a way of life impoverishes a human being, inflicting sometimes serious and always irreversible damage. Love as a kind of innocence and as a capacity for illusion, as an aptitude for epitomizing the whole of the other sex in a single loved being rarely resists a year of sexual immorality, and never two. In reality the successive sexual experiences accumulated during adolescence undermine and rapidly destroy all possibility of projection of an emotional and romantic sort; progressively, and in fact extremely quickly, one becomes as capable of love as an old slag. And so one leads, obviously, a slag's life; in ageing one becomes less seductive, and on that account bitter. One is jealous of the young, and so one hates them. Condemned to remain unavowable, this hatred festers and becomes increasingly fervent; then it dies down and fades away, just as everything fades away. All that remains is resentment and disgust, sickness and the anticipation of death.

At the bar I managed to negotiate a bottle of bourbon with the barman for seven hundred francs. On turning round I banged into a young six foot six electrician. 'Hey, what's your problem?' he said in a not unfriendly tone; gazing up at him, I replied 'The milk of human kindness.' I saw my face in the mirror; it was gripped by a clearly unpleasant rictus. The electrician shook his head in resignation; I negotiated the crossing of the dance floor, bottle in hand; just before arriving at my destination I bumped into a woman at the cash desk and fell to the floor. Nobody helped me up. I was seeing the dancers' legs pumping all around me; I wanted to chop them off with an axe. The lighting effects were of an unbearable violence; I was in hell.

A group of boys and girls were sitting at our table; probably the pseudo-Véronique's classmates. Tisserand wasn't giving in, although he was starting to be a bit out of it; he was letting himself be progressively edged out of the conversation, as was all too obvious; and when one of the boys proposed buying a round at the bar he was already implicitly excluded. He nevertheless made the vague gesture of getting up, he tried to catch pseudo-Véronique's eye; in vain. Thinking better of it, he let himself fall back heavily on the wall-sofa; completely huddled in on himself, he wasn't even aware of my presence; I poured myself another drink.

Tisserand's immobility was maintained for a minute or so; then he gave a sudden start, doubtless imputable to what is usually called 'the energy of despair'. Rising abruptly, he brushed past me as he made for the dance floor; his face was smiling and determined; he was still as ugly as ever, though.

Without hesitating he planted himself in front of a blond and very sexy girl of about fifteen. She was wearing a short and skimpy dress of an immaculate white; perspiration had glued it to her body, and it was visible that she had nothing on underneath; her little round buttocks were moulded with perfect precision; one could clearly make out, stiffened by excitement, the brown aureolae of her breasts; the disc jockey had just announced fifteen minutes of oldies.

Tisserand invited her to jive; taken rather unawares, she accepted. From the very first chords of *Come On Everybody* I sensed he was about to screw up. He was swinging the girl around brutally, teeth clenched, a vicious look to him; each time he pulled her towards him he took the opportunity to plant his hand on her buttocks. As soon as the last notes played the young girl rushed off towards a group of girls her own age. Tisserand remained resolutely in the middle of the floor; he was slobbering slightly. The girl was pointing to him while speaking to her chums; she guffawed as she looked his way.

At this moment the pseudo-Véronique returned from the bar with her group of friends; she was deep in conversation with a young black guy, or rather half black. He was slightly older than her; I reckoned he could be about twenty. They came and sat down near our table; as they passed I gave a friendly little wave of the hand to the pseudo-Véronique. She looked at me in surprise but didn't react.

After the second rock number the disc jockey put on a slow song. It was Nino Ferrer's *Le Sud*; a magnificent record, it has to be said. The half-caste touched the pseudo-Véronique's shoulder lightly; they got up of common accord. At this instant Tisserand turned to face him. He spread his hands, opened his mouth, but I don't think he can have had the time to speak. The half-caste eased him aside calmly, with gentleness, and in a few seconds they were on the dance floor.

They made a magnificent couple. The pseudo-

Véronique was quite tall, maybe five seven, but he was a good head taller. She confidently pressed her body against the guy's. Tisserand sat down again at my side; he was trembling in every limb. He watched the couple, hypnotized. I waited a minute or more; this slow dance, I recalled, went on forever. Then I shook him gently by the shoulder, repeating 'Raphaël' over and again.

—What can I do? he asked.

—Go and have a wank.

—You reckon it's hopeless?

—Sure. It's been hopeless for a long time, from the very beginning. You will never represent, Raphaël, a young girl's erotic dream. You have to resign yourself to the inevitable; such things are not for you. It's already too late, in any case. The sexual failure you've known since your adolescence, Raphaël, the frustration that has followed you since the age of thirteen, will leave their indelible mark. Even supposing that you might have women in the future – which in all frankness I doubt – this will not be enough; nothing will ever be enough. You will always be an orphan to those adolescent loves you never knew. In you the wound is already deep; it will get deeper and deeper. An atrocious, unremitting bitterness will end up gripping your heart. For you there will be neither redemption nor deliverance. That's how it is. Yet that doesn't mean, however, that all possibility of revenge is closed to you. These women you desire so much, you too can possess them. You can even possess what is most precious about them. What is it, Raphaël, that is most precious about them?

—Their beauty? he suggested.

—It's not their beauty, I can tell you that much; it isn't

their vagina either, nor even their love; because all these disappear with life itself. And from now on you can possess their life. Launch yourself on a career of murder this very evening; believe me, my friend, it's the only way still open to you. When you feel these women trembling at the end of your knife, and begging for their young lives, then will you truly be the master; then will you possess them body and soul. Perhaps you will even manage, prior to their sacrifice, to obtain various succulent favours from them; a knife, Raphaël, is a powerful ally.

He was staring long and hard at the couple who were intertwined as they slowly turned around the dance floor; one of the pseudo-Véronique's hands encircled the half-caste's waist, the other was resting on his shoulder. Softly, almost timidly, he said to me, 'I'd rather kill the guy.' I knew then that I'd won; I suddenly relaxed and refilled our glasses.

—Well then, I exclaimed, what's stopping you? Why yes! Get the hang of it on a young nigger! In any case they're going to leave together, the thing looks cut and dried. You'll have, of course, to kill the guy before getting a piece of the woman. As it happens I've a knife in the front of the car.

They did in fact leave together ten minutes later. I got up, grabbing the bottle as I did; Tisserand followed me docilely.

Outside, the night was oddly pleasant, warm almost. There was a brief conflab in the parking lot between the girl and the black guy; they made off towards a scooter. I got into the front of the car, took the knife out of its bag; its serrations gleamed prettily in the moonlight. Before getting on the scooter they embraced for some time; it was beautiful and very tender. By my side Tisserand was trembling incessantly; I had the feeling I could smell the putrid sperm rising in his prick. Playing nervously with the controls, he dipped the headlights; the girl blinked. They decided then to leave; our car moved off gently behind them. Tisserand asked me:

—Where are they going to sleep?

—Probably at the girl's parents; it's the done thing. But we'll have to stop them before then. As soon as we're on a back road we'll run into the scooter. They'll probably be a bit banged up; you won't have any problem finishing off the guy.

The car was bowling smoothly along the coast road; ahead, in the beam of the headlights, the girl could be seen clutching the waist of her companion. After a few minutes' silence I started in again:

—We could always drive over them, just to be on the safe side.

—They don't look to be concerned about anything, he remarked in a dreamy voice.

Suddenly the scooter veered off to the right along a track going down to the sea. This wasn't in the plan; I told Tisserand to slow down. A bit further on the couple pulled up; I noticed that the guy was taking the trouble to set his anti-theft device before leading the girl off towards the dunes.

Once over the first lot of dunes I understood more. Almost at high tide, and forming an immense curve, the sea extended to our feet; the light of the full moon was playing gently on its surface. The couple were making off towards the south, skirting the edge of the water. The air temperature was increasingly pleasant, abnormally pleasant; you'd have thought it was the month of June. In these conditions, well sure, I understood: to make love beside the ocean, under the splendour of the stars; I understood only too well; it's exactly what I'd have done in their place. I proffered the knife to Tisserand; he left without a word.

I went back towards the car; supporting myself on the hood, I slid down on to the sand. I gulped down a few mouthfuls of bourbon, then got behind the wheel and steered the car in the direction of the sea. It was a bit risky, but the sound of the engine itself seemed muffled, imperceptible; the night was all-embracing, tender. I had a terrible yearning to drive straight into the ocean. Tisserand's absence was becoming prolonged.

When he returned he didn't say a word. He was holding the long knife in his hand; the blade was glinting softly; I detected no bloodstains on its surface. All of a sudden I felt a wave of sadness. Finally, he spoke.

—When I got there they were lying between two dunes. He'd already taken her dress and her bra off. Her breasts were so beautiful, so round in the moonlight. Then she turned, she lay on top of him. She unbuttoned his trousers. When she began sucking him off I couldn't stand it.

He fell silent. I waited. The sea was as smooth as a lake.

—I turned back, I walked between the dunes. I could have killed them; they were oblivious to everything, they didn't even know I was there. I masturbated. I had no wish to kill them; blood changes nothing.

—Blood is everywhere.

—I know. Sperm is everywhere too. Right now I've had enough. I'm going back to Paris.

He didn't suggest that I accompany him. I got up, walked towards the sea. The bottle of bourbon was almost empty; I swallowed the last mouthful. When I got back the beach was deserted; I hadn't even heard the car drive off.

I was never to see Tisserand again; he was killed in his car that night, on his return trip to Paris. There was a lot of fog on the outskirts of Angers; he was driving like the clappers, as usual. His 205 GTI collided head-on with a lorry that had pulled out into the middle of the carriageway. He died instantly, just before dawn. The next day was a holiday, to celebrate the birth of Christ; it was only three days later that his family heard about the business. The burial had already taken place, according to ritual; which cut short any idea of wreaths or mourners. A few words were pronounced on the sadness of such a death and on the difficulty of driving in fog, people went back to work, and that was that.

At least, I said to myself on learning of his death, he'll have battled to the end. The Under-25s club, the winter sports vacations . . . At least he won't have abdicated, won't have thrown in the towel. Right to the end, and despite repeated failure, he'll have looked for love. Squashed flat in the bodywork of his 205 GTI on the almost deserted highway, all bloody in his black suit and gold tie, I know that in his heart there was still the struggle, the desire and the will to struggle.

Part Three

1

Ah yes, that was unconscious irony*! One breathes freely . . .*

After Tisserand's departure I slept fitfully; doubtless I masturbated. On awakening my tackle was sticky, the sand damp and cold; frankly I'd had enough. I was sorry Tisserand hadn't killed the black guy; day was breaking.

I was miles away from any village. I got up and set off down the road. What else was there for it? My cigarettes were sodden but still smokable.

On returning to Paris I found a letter emanating from the ex-pupils' association of my engineering school; it suggested I buy fine wines and foie gras for the holidays, all at unbeatable prices. I remarked to myself that the mailout had been done with intolerable lateness.

The next day I didn't go to work. For no precise reason; I simply didn't fancy it. Squatting on the moquette I leafed through some mail order catalogues. In a brochure put out by the Galeries Lafayette I found an interesting description of human beings, under the title *Today's People*:

After a really full day they snuggle down into a deep sofa with sober lines (Steiner, Roset, Cinna). *To a jazz tune they admire the style of their Dhurries carpets, the gaiety of their wall coverings* (Patrick Frey). *Ready to set off for a frenzied set of tennis, towels await them in the bathroom* (Yves Saint-Laurent, Ted Lapidus). *And it's before a dinner with intimate friends in their kitchens created by* Daniel Hechter *or* Primrose Bordier *that they'll remake the world.*

Friday and Saturday I didn't do much; let's just say I meditated, if you can call it that. I remember having thought of suicide, of its paradoxical usefulness. Let's put a chimpanzee in a tiny cage fronted by concrete bars. The animal would go berserk, throw itself against the walls, rip out its hair, inflict cruel bites on itself, and in 73% of cases will actually end up killing itself. Let's now make a breach in one of the walls, which we will place right next to a bottomless precipice. Our friendly sample quadrumane will approach the edge, he'll look down, remain at the edge for ages, return there time and again, but generally he won't teeter over the brink; and in all events his nervous state will be radically assuaged.

My meditation on chimpanzees was prolonged late into the night of Saturday and Sunday, and I finished up laying the foundations for an animal story called *Dialogues Between a Chimpanzee and a Stork*, which in fact constituted a political pamphlet of rare violence. Taken prisoner by a tribe of storks, the chimpanzee was at first self-preoccupied, his thoughts far away. One morning, summoning up his courage, he demanded to see the eldest of the storks. Immediately brought before the bird, he raised his arms dramatically to the sky before pronouncing this despairing discourse:

'Of all economic and social systems, capitalism is

unquestionably the most natural. This already suffices to show that it is bound to be the worst. Once this conclusion is drawn it only remains to develop a workable and consistent set of concepts, that is, one whose mechanical functioning will permit, proceeding from facts introduced by chance, the generation of multiple proofs which reinforce the predetermined judgment, the way that bars of graphite can reinforce the structure of a nuclear reactor. That is a simple task, worthy of a very young monkey; however I would like to disregard it.

'During the migration of the spermatic flood towards the neck of the uterus, an imposing phenomenon, completely respectable and absolutely essential for the reproduction of species, one sometimes observes the aberrant comportment of certain spermatozoa. They look ahead, they look behind, they sometimes even swim against the current for a few brief seconds, and the accelerated wriggling of their tail now seems to translate as the revising of an ontological decision. If they do not compensate for this surprising indecision by a given velocity they generally arrive too late, and consequently rarely participate at the grand festival of genetic recombination. And so it was in August 1793 that Maximilien Robespierre was carried along by the movement of history like a crystal of chalcedony caught in a distant avalanche, or better still like a young stork with still too-feeble wings, born by unhappy chance just before the approach of winter, and which suffers considerable difficulty – the thing is understandable – in maintaining a correct course during the crossing of jet-streams. Now jet-streams are, as we know, particularly violent on the approaches of Africa. But I shall refine my thinking once more.

'On the day of his execution Maximilien Robespierre had a broken jaw. It was held together by a bandage. Just before placing his head under the blade the executioner wrenched off his bandage; Robespierre let out a scream of pain, torrents of blood spurted from his wound, his broken teeth spilled forth on the ground. Then the executioner brandished the bandage at the end of his arm like a trophy, showing it to the crowd massed around the scaffold. People were laughing, jeering.

'At this point the chroniclers generally add: "The Revolution was over." This is rigorously exact.

'At the very moment the executioner brandished his disgusting blood-soaked bandage to the acclaim of the crowd, I like to think that in the mind of Robespierre there was something other than suffering. Something apart from the feeling of failure. A hope? Or doubtless the feeling that he'd done what he had to do. Maximilien Robespierre, I love you.'

The eldest stork replied simply, in a slow and terrible voice: *Tat twam asi*. Shortly afterwards the chimpanzee was executed by the tribe of storks; he died in atrocious pain, transpierced and emasculated by their pointed beaks. For having questioned the order of the world the chimpanzee had to perish; in fact one could understand it; really, that's how it was.

On Sunday morning I went out for a while in the neighbourhood; I bought some raisin bread. The day was warm but a little sad, as Sundays often are in Paris, especially when one doesn't believe in God.

2

The following Monday I went back to my job, a bit on the off chance. I knew my head of department had taken between Christmas and New Year's Day off; probably to go skiing in the Alps. I thought there'd be nobody there, that nobody would feel in the least bit like me, and that my day would be spent tapping idly away on some keyboard. Around eleven-thirty, unfortunately, some guy spots me, knows who I am. He introduces himself as my new immediate superior; I have no wish to doubt his word. He has the air of being more or less up on my activities, though in a very vague way. He also tries to make contact, to be friendly; I don't succumb to his advances in the least.

At midday, partly out of desperation, I went to eat with a business manager and a managerial secretary. I was of a mind to converse with them, but wasn't given the opportunity; they seemed to be pursuing an already ancient conversation:

—I finally got twenty-watt speakers for my car stereo, bragged the business manager. The ten watts appeared a bit weak and thirty watts was really much more expensive. I reckon it's not worth it just for the car.

—Personally, the secretary retorted, I've had four speakers put in, two in the front and two in the back.

The business manager contrived a ribald smile. So that was it, everything was proceeding as normal.

I spent the afternoon in my office doing various things; more or less nothing in fact. From time to time I consulted my diary: we were at 29 December. It was essential I do something for the 31st. People do something, for the 31st.

In the evening I phone SOS Amitié, but the line's busy, like it always is during the holiday period. Around one in the morning I take a tin of petits pois and hurl it at the bathroom mirror. That makes for a nice lot of glass splinters. I cut myself picking them up and start bleeding. This pleases me. It's just what I wanted.

The next day I'm in my office by eight. My new immediate superior is already there; has the idiot slept in the place? A grimy mist of unpleasant aspect floats above the esplanade between the towerblocks. The fluorescent lights of the offices through which the COMATEC employees pass to do the cleaning go on and off by turns, creating the impression of life unfolding in slow motion. The immediate superior offers me a coffee; he hasn't, it seems, given up on trying to win me over. Stupidly I accept, which means that before a few minutes are up I find myself being given a somewhat delicate task: the detection of errors in a *software package* that has just been sold to the Ministry of Industry. There are, it appears, some errors. I spend two hours on it, and as far as I can tell there aren't any; it's true that my mind is elsewhere.

Around ten we learn of the death of Tisserand. A call from the family which a secretary passes on to the whole staff. We will receive, she says, a formal announcement later. I can't really believe it; it's too nightmarish for words. But no, it's all true.

A little later in the morning I get a phone call from Catherine Lechardoy. She has nothing in particular to say. 'Maybe we'll see each other again,' she opines; I rather doubt it.

Around midday I went out. In the bookshop on the square I bought number 80 of the Michelin map (*Rodez–Albi–Nîmes*). Once back in my office I scrutinized it carefully. Around five I came to the conclusion that I must go to Saint-Cirgues-en-Montagne. The name stood out, in splendid isolation, amid forests and little triangles representing mountaintops; there wasn't a single conurbation within a radius of thirty kilometres. I sensed I was on the edge of making a vital discovery; that a revelation of the highest order was awaiting me down there, between the 31st of December and the first of January, at the precise moment the year turns. I left a note on my desk: 'Left early due to the train strike'. On thinking about it I left a second note announcing, in block capitals: 'I AM SICK'. And I returned home, not without some difficulty: the Paris Transport Authority strike, begun that morning, had spread; there was no more métro, just a few buses, depending on the route.

The Gare de Lyon was practically in a state of siege. Patrols of CRS riot police were cordoning off areas in the entrance hall and circulating along the platforms; the word was that squads of 'hard' strikers had decided to prevent all departures. Nevertheless the train turned out to be almost empty, and the trip completely trouble-free.

At Lyon-Perrache station an impressive number of buses were being laid on for Morzine, La Clusaz, Courchevel, Val d'Isère. For the Ardèche, nothing like. I took a taxi to the Part-Dieu bus station, where I spent a fastidious quarter of an hour browsing through a malfunctioning electronic timetable before finally discovering that a coach was leaving at 6.45 the next morning for Aubenas; it was half-past midnight. I decided to spend those few hours in Lyon Part-Dieu; I was probably making a big mistake. Above the bus station proper rises a hypermodern structure in glass and steel, with four or five levels linked by stainless steel escalators which are activated at the least approach; nothing save luxury shops (perfume and cosmetics, haute couture, gadgets) with absurdly aggressive window displays; nothing for sale that might prove remotely useful. All around there are monitors which broadcast pop promos and adverts; and, of course, permanent background music consisting of the latest Top 50 hits. At night the building is invaded by a gang of vagrants and semi-derelicts. Filthy, wretched creatures, brutish and completely dull-witted, who live in blood, hate, and their own excrement. They gather at night, like huge flies on shit, around the deserted luxury shops. They move in packs, the solitude in this place being all but fatal. They remain in front of the video monitors, blankly absorbing the advertising images. Sometimes they strike up a quarrel, get their knives out. From time to time a dead body is found in the morning, throat cut by his mates.

I strolled all night among the creatures. I was completely unafraid. Partly out of provocation, I even made a show of drawing out all the money remaining on my Visa from a cashpoint. One thousand four hundred francs in notes. A handsome prize. They watched me, watched me long and hard, but no one tried to speak to me or even get any closer than three metres.

Around six in the morning I gave up on my plan; I took a TGV in the afternoon.

The night of 31 December will be hard. I feel as if things are falling apart within me, like so many glass partitions shattering. I walk from place to place in the grip of a fury, needing to act, yet can do nothing about it because any attempt seems doomed in advance. Failure, everywhere failure. Only suicide hovers above me, gleaming and inaccessible.

Around midnight I feel something like a muted parting of the ways; there's something painful going on inside. I no longer understand anything.

A clear improvement on January the first. My state approaches something like stupor; this is no bad thing.

In the afternoon I make an appointment with a psychiatrist. There's a system of urgent psychiatric appointments by Minitel; you tap in your schedule, they supply you with the practitioner. All very practical.

Mine is called Doctor Népote. He lives in the 6th arrondissement; like a lot of psychiatrists, I get the feeling. I arrive at his place at 7.30. The fellow looks like a psychiatrist to a striking degree. His library is impeccably arranged; there's neither African mask nor first edition of *Sexus*; he's not a psychoanalyst, then. On the other hand it looks like he subscribes to *Synpase*. This seems an excellent omen.

The episode of the abortive trip to the Ardèche appears to interest him. With a bit of digging, he succeeds in making me admit that my parents were Ardéchois in origin. So now he's on the track: according to him I'm in search of 'signs of identity'. All my shiftings about, he generalizes audaciously, are so many 'quests for identity'. It's possible; I rather doubt it, though. My professional trips, for example, are obviously something imposed on me. But I don't want to discuss it. He has a theory, which is fine by me. After all it's always better to have a theory.

Somewhat bizarrely, he goes on to question me about my work. I don't get it; I'm unable to grant his question real importance. That's clearly not the issue here.

He defines his thinking precisely, in speaking to me of the 'possibilities for social rapport' offered by the job. I burst out laughing, much to his surprise. He gives me another appointment for Monday.

The next morning I phone my company to say I've had a 'slight relapse'. They seem mightily pissed-off about it.

A weekend without drama; I sleep a lot. It astonishes me that I'm only thirty; I feel much older.

3

The first incident, the following Monday, occurred around two p.m. I saw the guy approaching a long way off, I felt a slight wave of sadness. It was someone I liked, a nice man, though highly unfortunate. I knew he was divorced, that he'd been living alone with his daughter for some time now. I also knew he was drinking a bit too much. I had no wish to mix him up in all this.

He came up to me, said hello and asked me for details of a programme that apparently I should know about. I burst into sobs. He beat a hasty retreat, nonplussed, a bit bewildered; he even apologized, I think. He really had no need to apologize, the poor sod.

I ought to have left right then, obviously; we were alone in the office, there'd been no witnesses, the whole thing could still be sorted out in a relatively decent manner.

The second incident occurred around an hour later. This time the office was full of people. A girl came in, cast a disapproving glance at the assembled company and finally chose to address herself to me, to tell me I was smoking too much, that it was insupportable, that I clearly had no regard for others. I replied with a pair of slaps to the face. She looked at me, she too slightly bewildered. Evidently she wasn't used to this; I surmised that she couldn't have received enough smacks as a kid. For a second I wondered if she wasn't going to slap me in return; I knew that if she did I'd burst into sobs right away.

There's a pause, then she says, 'But . . .', her lower jaw idiotically agape. By now everyone has turned towards us. A tremendous silence has descended on the office. I turn away and in a loud voice I proclaim, to nobody in particular, 'I've got an appointment with a psychiatrist!' and I leave. The death of a professional.

Besides it's true, I do have an appointment with the psychiatrist, but there are still something like three hours to go. I will spend them in a fast food joint, shredding the cardboard packaging of my hamburger. Without real method, so that the final result proves disappointing. A shredding pure and simple.

Once I've recounted my little fantasies to the practitioner he puts me on leave of absence for a week. He even asks me if I wouldn't like to take a short break in a rest home. I reply that no thanks, I'm afraid of mad people.

A week later I go back to see him. I've nothing much to say; I do manage a few sentences, though. Reading his spiral notebook upside-down I see he's jotted 'ideational decline'. Huh, huh. According to him, then, I seem to be on the way to becoming an imbecile. It's a theory.

From time to time he glances at his wristwatch (fawn leather strap, rectangular gold-plated face); I get the feeling of not overly interesting him. I ask myself if he keeps a revolver in his drawer, for patients in a state of violent crisis. At the end of half an hour he pronounces a few phrases of general import on periods of blankness, extends my leave of absence and increases my dosage of medication. He also reveals that my condition has a name: it's a depression. Officially, then, I'm in a depression. The formula seems a happy one to me. It's not that I feel tremendously low; it's rather that the world around me appears high.

The next morning I go back to my office; my head of department wishes to see me to 'take stock'. As I expected, he has returned from his stay in Val d'Isère extremely suntanned; but I make out a few fine wrinkles at the corners of his eyes; he is a little less handsome than my recollection of him. I don't know why, but I'm disappointed.

I inform him right away that I'm *in a depression*; he is stunned, then recovers. After this the conversation drones on pleasantly for half an hour, but I know that from now on it's as if there's an invisible wall between us. He will never again consider me as an equal, nor as a possible successor; in his eyes I no longer even really exist; I have forfeited all rights. In any case I know they're going to get rid of me as soon as my two months of legal sick leave are up; it's what they always do in cases of depression; I've seen it happen before.

Within the limits of these constraints he acquits himself rather well, he tries to make excuses for me. At a certain moment he comes out with:

—In this line of work we are sometimes put under terrible pressure . . .

—Oh, not really, I reply.

He gives a start as if he were waking up, brings the

conversation to an end. He will make one last effort and accompany me to the door, yet keeping at a safe distance of two metres, as if he were afraid I might suddenly puke all over him. He ends with, 'Well, get some rest then, take all the time you need.'

I leave. Here I am, a free man.

4

The Confession of Jean-Pierre Buvet

The subsequent weeks have left me the memory of a gradual decline, interspersed with acutely painful phases. Apart from the psychiatrist I was seeing nobody; I was going out after nightfall to buy cigarettes and sliced bread. One Saturday evening, though, I received a phone call from Jean-Pierre Buvet; he seemed tense.

—Well? Still a priest? I said to de-ice the atmosphere.

—I'd like to see you.

—Sure, we could see each other.

—Now, if you can.

I'd never set foot inside his house before; all I knew was that he lived in Vitry. The council block, moreover, was well kept. Two young Arabs followed me with their eyes, one of them spat on the ground as I went by. At least he hadn't spat in my face.

The apartment was paid for by funds from the diocese, something of the kind. Collapsed in front of his TV set, Buvet was casting a dejected eye at *Holy Eventide*. He'd knocked back quite a few beers while waiting for me, it appeared.

—What's up, then? I asked good-naturedly.

—I'd told you Vitry wasn't an easy parish; it's even worse than you can imagine. Since my arrival I've tried to set up kids' groups; no kids ever came. It's three months now since I've celebrated a baptism. At mass I've never managed more than five people: four Africans and an old Breton woman; I believe she was eighty-two, an ex-employee of the railways. She'd been widowed for ages; her children didn't come to see her any more, she no longer had their address. One Sunday I didn't see her at mass. I passed by her house, she lives in a high-priority housing area over there . . . (He made a vague gesture, can in hand, dousing the carpet with beer). Her neighbours told me she'd just been attacked; they'd taken her off to hospital, but she only had slight fractures. I visited her; her fractures were taking time to mend, of course, but there was no danger. When I went back a week later she was dead. I asked for explanations, the doctors refused to give me any. They'd already cremated her; nobody in the family had bothered to attend. I'm certain she'd have wished for a religious burial; she hadn't said as much to me, she never spoke of death; but I'm certain that's what she'd have wanted.

He took a swig, then went on:

—Three days later I received a visit from Patricia.

There was a significant pause. I shot a glance at the TV screen. The sound was turned down; a singer in a black and gold g-string appeared to be surrounded by pythons, or even anacondas. Then I returned my gaze to Buvet, while trying to communicate a grimace of sympathy. He went on:

—She wished to make confession, but she didn't know how, she didn't know the procedure. Patricia was a nurse in the department where they'd taken the old woman; she'd heard the doctors talking among themselves. They didn't want to have her occupying a bed during the months necessary for her recovery; they were saying she was an unnecessary burden. So they decided to give her a lytic cocktail; that's a mixture of high-dose tranquillizers that brings about a quick and peaceful death. They discussed it for two minutes, no more; then the head of the department came to ask Patricia to administer the injection. She did it the same night. It's the first time she's performed a euthanasia; but her colleagues often do it. She died very fast, in her sleep. After that Patricia was unable to sleep; she was dreaming of the old woman.

—What have you done about it?

—I went to the archdiocese; they knew the whole story. A lot of euthanasias are performed in that hospital, apparently. There have never been any complaints; in any case, up to now all the trials have ended in acquittals.

He fell silent, finished his beer in one go, opened another can; then, taking his courage in his hands, he pressed on:

—For a month now I've seen Patricia practically every night. I don't know what's taken hold of me. Since the seminary I've not suffered from temptation. She was so kind, so naive. She knew nothing about religious matters, she was extremely curious about it all. She didn't understand why priests don't have the right to make love. She wondered if they had a sex life, if they masturbated. I replied to all her questions, I didn't feel any embarrassment. I was praying a lot during this period, I was constantly rereading the Gospels; I didn't have the feeling of doing anything wrong; I sensed that Christ understood me, that He was with me.

He fell silent once more. On the TV screen now there was an ad for the Renault Clio. The car looked ultra-comfortable.

—Last Monday Patricia announced to me that she'd met another guy. In a discothèque, the Metropolis. She told me we wouldn't see each other again, but that she was glad to have known me; she really liked changing boyfriends; she was only twenty. Basically she liked me a lot, but no more than that; it was mainly the idea of sleeping with a priest that excited her, that she found droll; but she wouldn't say anything to anybody, that was a promise.

This time the silence was to last two minutes or more. I asked myself what a psychologist would have said in my place; probably nothing. Finally an absurd thought came to me:

—You should go and confess.

—Tomorrow I must say mass. I don't see how I can do it. I don't think I can cope. I no longer feel the presence.

—What presence?

After that we didn't say much. From time to time I was uttering phrases like 'Oh, come on, come on'; he continued regularly putting away the beers. Clearly I could do nothing for him. In the end I called a taxi.

As I was crossing the threshold he said to me, 'See you soon.' I don't believe it for a moment. I get the feeling we'll never see each other again.

It's freezing in my place. I remember that earlier in the

evening, just before leaving, I smashed a window with a blow of the fist. Yet, oddly, my hand is intact; no cuts.

I lie down even so, and I sleep. The nightmares will only appear much later in the night. Not instantly recognizable as nightmares; even rather pleasant.

I am gliding over Chartres Cathedral. I have a mystical vision concerning Chartres Cathedral. It seems to hold and to symbolize a secret – an ultimate secret. During all this time groups of nuns are forming in the gardens by the side entrances. They greet the old and even the dying, explaining to them that I am going to unveil a secret.

Meanwhile I am walking down the corridors of a hospital. A man has given me an appointment, but he isn't there. I must wait a moment in a refrigerated storeroom, then I reach a new corridor. He still isn't there, the man who could get me out of hospital. Then I attend an exhibition. It's Patrick Leroy from the Ministry of Agriculture who's organized it all. He has cut people's heads out of some illustrated periodicals, stuck them on to various paintings (representing, for instance, Triassic flora), and is selling his little figurines very expensively. I have the feeling he wants me to buy one; he has a self-satisfied, almost menacing air.

Then I'm flying once again over Chartres Cathedral. The cold is extreme. I am absolutely alone. My wings easily bear me up.

I am nearing some towers, but I no longer recognize anything. These towers are immense, black, maleficent, they are made of black marble which emits a harsh glare, the marble is encrusted with violently coloured figurines in which the horrors of organic life are glaringly apparent.

I fall, I fall between the towers. My face, which is going to be smashed to smithereens, is covered over with lines of blood which precisely delineate the location of the fractures. My nose is a gaping hole from which organic matter oozes.

And now I am on the deserted plains of Champagne. There are tiny snowflakes flying all about, along with pages from an illustrated periodical, printed in huge screaming type. The periodical must date from around 1900.

Am I a reporter or journalist? It would seem so, since the style of the articles is familiar to me. They are written in that tone of bitter lament dear to the anarchists and surrealists.

Octavie Léoncet, ninety-two, has been found murdered in her barn. A little farm in the Vosges. Her sister, Léontine Léoncet, eighty-seven, takes pleasure in showing the corpse to journalists. The crime weapons are there, clearly visible: a wood saw and a brace and bit. Everything blood-stained, of course.

And the crimes are on the increase. Always old women isolated on their farms. On each occasion the young and elusive murderer leaves the tools of his trade in evidence: sometimes a burin, sometimes a pair of secateurs, sometimes simply a small hand saw.

And all this is magical, adventurous, libertarian.

I wake up. It is cold. I dive back into the dream.

Each time, faced with these blood-stained tools, I experience the sufferings of the victim in gruesome detail. Soon I have an erection. There are some scissors on the table near my bed. The idea comes to me: to cut off my penis. I imagine myself with the pair of scissors in my hand, the slight resistance of the flesh, and suddenly the bloody stump, the probable fainting.

The sectioned end on the moquette. Matted with blood.

Around eleven I wake up once again. I have two pairs of scissors, one in each room. I go and fetch them and place them under several books. It is an effort of will, probably insufficient. The need persists, increases and evolves. This time my plan is to take a pair of scissors, plant them in my eyes and tear them out. More precisely in the left eye, in a place I know well, there where it seems so hollow in the socket.

And then I take some sedatives, and everything's dandy. Everything's dandy.

5

Venus and Mars

Following that night I thought it wise to reconsider Doctor Népote's suggestion about staying in a rest home. He warmly congratulated me on this. According to him, I was thereby taking the shortest road to a complete recovery. The fact that the initiative might come from me was highly positive; I was beginning to take responsibility for my own cure. This was good; this was even very good.

So, provided with his letter of introduction, I presented myself at Rueil-Malmaison. There was a park, and the meals were taken communally. In point of fact all ingestion of solid food was impossible for me at first; I was vomiting it up straightaway, with painful hiccups; I had the feeling my teeth were going to leave with it. It was necessary to resort to perfusions.

Colombian in origin, the chief doctor was of little help to me. With the imperturbable seriousness of the neurotic, I was putting forward incontrovertible arguments against my survival; the least among them seemed enough to warrant instant suicide. He appeared to listen; at all events he remained silent; occasionally it was all he could do to stifle a slight yawn. It was only after a number of weeks that the truth dawned on me: I was speaking softly; he only had a very approximate knowledge of the French language; in effect he didn't understand a word of my stories.

Slightly older, more modest in social origin, the psychologist who assisted him did on the other hand give me much-needed help. It's true that she was compiling a thesis on anxiety, and so was in need of data. She used a Radiola tape-recorder; she asked my permission to turn it on. Naturally I said yes. I rather liked her chapped hands, her bitten nails, as she pressed *Record*. Nevertheless, I've always hated female psychology students: vile creatures, that's how I perceive them. But this older woman, who looked like she'd been through a wringer, face framed by a turban, almost inspired my confidence.

At first, though, our relations were not easy. She took me to task for speaking in general, overly sociological, terms. This, according to her, was not interesting: instead I ought to involve myself, try and 'get myself centred'.

—But I've had a bellyful of myself, I objected.

—As a psychologist I can't accept such a statement, nor encourage it in any way. In speaking of society all the time you create a barrier behind which you can hide; it's up to me to break down this barrier so that we can work on your personal problems.

This dialogue of the deaf went on for a little over two months. I think that basically she liked me well enough. I remember one morning, it was already the beginning of Spring; through the window birds could be seen, hopping on the lawn. She was looking fresh and relaxed.

First off, there was a brief conversation about the dosage of my medication; then in a direct, spontaneous, completely unexpected way she asked me: 'Basically, why is it you're so unhappy?' It was something totally unexpected, this frankness. And I too did something unexpected: I proffered her a short text I'd written the night before to occupy my insomnia.

—I'd prefer to hear you speak, she said.

—Read it all the same.

'Early on certain individuals experience the frightening impossibility of living by themselves; basically they cannot bear to see their own life before them, to see it in its entirety without areas of shadow, without substance. Their existence is I admit an exception to the laws of nature, not only because this fracture of basic maladjustment is produced outside of any genetic finality but also by dint of the excessive lucidity it presupposes, an obviously transcendent lucidity in relation to the perceptual schemas of ordinary existence. It is sometimes enough to place another individual before them, providing he is taken to be as pure, as transparent as they are themselves, for this insupportable fracture to resolve itself as a luminous, tense and permanent aspiration towards the absolutely inaccessible. Thus, while day after day a mirror only returns the same desperate image, two parallel mirrors elaborate and edify a clear and dense system which draws the human eye into an infinite, unbounded trajectory, infinite in its geometrical purity, beyond all suffering and beyond the world.'

I raised my eyes, looked her way. She had a somewhat astonished air. Finally she came out with: 'That's interesting, the mirror . . '. She must have read something in Freud, or in *The Mickey Mouse Annual*. In the last analysis she was doing what she could, she was kind. Plucking up courage, she added:

—But I'd prefer that you spoke directly of your problems. Once again you're being too abstract.

—Maybe. But I don't understand, basically, how people manage to go on living. I get the impression everybody must be unhappy; we live in such a simple world, you understand. There's a system based on domination, money and fear – a somewhat masculine system, let's call it Mars; there's a feminine system based on seduction and sex, Venus let's say. And that's it. Is it really possible to live and to believe that there's nothing else? Along with the late nineteenth-century realists, Maupassant believed there was nothing else; and it drove him completely mad.

—You're mixing everything up. Maupassant's madness was only a classic stage in the development of syphilis. Any normal human being accepts the two systems you're talking about.

—No. If Maupassant went mad it's because he had an acute awareness of matter, of nothingness and death – and that he had no awareness of anything else. Alike in this to our contemporaries, he established an absolute separation between his individual existence and the rest of the world. It's the only way in which we can conceive the world today. For example, a bullet from a .45 Magnum may graze my cheek and end up hitting the wall behind me; I'll be unscathed. Taking the opposite example, the bullet will splatter my flesh, my physical suffering will be enormous; at the end of the day my face will be disfigured; perhaps the eye will be splattered too, in which case I'll be both disfigured and blind; from then on I'll inspire repugnance in other men. At a more general level, we are all subject to ageing and to death. This notion of ageing and death is insupportable for the individual human being; in the kind of civilization we live in it develops in a sovereign and unconditional manner, it gradually occupies the whole field of consciousness, it allows nothing else to subsist. In this way, and little by little, knowledge of the world's constraints is established. Desire itself disappears; only bitterness, jealousy and fear remain. Above all there remains bitterness; an immense and inconceivable bitterness. No civilization, no epoch has been capable of developing such a quantity of bitterness in its subjects. In that sense we are living through unprecedented times. If it was necessary to sum up the contemporary mental state in a word, that's the one I'd undoubtedly choose: bitterness.

She didn't reply at first, thought for a few seconds, then asked me:

—When did you last have sexual relations?

—Just over two years ago.

—Ah! she exclaimed, almost in triumph. There you are then! Given that, how can you possibly feel good about life? . . .

—Would you be willing to make love with me?

She was flustered, I think she even blushed a bit. She was forty, thin and very much the worse for wear; but that morning she appeared really charming to me. I have a very tender memory of that moment. She was smiling, somewhat despite herself; I even thought she was going to say yes. But finally she collected herself:

—That's not my role. As a psychologist my role is to

equip you to undertake the process of seduction so that you might again have normal relations with young women.

For the remaining sessions she had herself replaced by a male colleague.

It was around about this time that I began taking an interest in my companions in misery. There were few deranged types, mainly sufferers from depression and anxiety; I suppose that was deliberate. People who experience these kinds of states quickly give up drawing attention to themselves. On the whole they remain lying down all day with their tranquillizers; from time to time they take a turn in the corridor, smoke four or five cigarettes, one after the other, then go back to bed. Meals, however, constituted a collective moment; the nurse on duty used to say 'Help yourselves.' No other word was uttered; each person chewed his food. Sometimes one of the inmates was overcome by a fit of trembling, or began to sob; he went back to his room, and that was that. The idea gradually dawned on me that all these people – men or women – were not in the least deranged; they were simply lacking in love. Their gestures, their attitudes, their dumb show betrayed an excruciating craving for physical contact and caresses; but that wasn't possible, of course. So they sobbed, emitted cries, lacerated themselves with their nails; during my stay we had a successful attempt at castration.

As the weeks went by my conviction grew that I was there to accomplish some pre-arranged plan – a bit like how in the Gospels Christ accomplishes what the prophets had already announced. At the same time the intuition was dawning that this stay was just the first in a succession of progressively longer internments in increasingly closed and tougher psychiatric establishments. The idea saddened me enormously.

I saw the psychologist from time to time in the corridor, but no real interchange came about; our relations had taken a highly formal turn. Her work on anxiety was progressing, she told me; she had to take some exams in June.

Doubtless I have some vague existence today in a doctoral dissertation, alongside other real-life cases. The thought of having become an item in a file calms me. I imagine the volume, its cloth binding, its slightly sad cover; I gently flatten myself between the pages; I am squashed.

I left the clinic on 26th of May; I recall the sunshine, the heat, the atmosphere of freedom in the streets. It was unbearable.

It was also on a 26th of May that I'd been conceived, late in the afternoon. The coitus had taken place in the living room, on a fake Pakistani rug. At the moment my father took my mother from behind she'd had the unfortunate idea of stretching out a hand and caressing him on the testicles, so adroitly that ejaculation was produced. She'd felt pleasure, but not true orgasm. They'd eaten cold chicken afterwards. That was thirty-two years ago now; at that time you could still find real chicken.

On the subject of my life, post-clinic, I had no precise instructions; I just had to show up once a week. The rest of the time it was, however, up to me to look after myself.

6

Saint-Cirgues-en-Montagne

> *As paradoxical as it may seem, there is a road to travel and it must be travelled, yet there is no traveller. Acts are accomplished, yet there is no actor.*
>
> — Sattipathana–Sutta, XLII, 16

On 20 June of the same year, I got up at six a.m. and turned on the radio, Radio Nostalgie to be exact. There was a song by Marcel Amont which spoke of a swarthy Mexican: light, carefree, a bit silly; exactly what I needed. I got washed listening to the radio, then collected a few things together. I'd decided to go back to Saint-Cirgues-en-Montagne; at least, to have another stab at it.

Before setting off, I finish what there is left to eat in the house. This is somewhat difficult as I'm not hungry. Fortunately there isn't much: four biscuits and a tin of sardines. I don't know why I'm doing it, it's obvious that these products keep. But it's been a while since the meaning of my actions has seemed clear to me; they don't seem clear very often, let's say. The rest of the time I'm more or less *in the position of observer*.

★

On entering the compartment I'm aware, even so, that I'm gradually losing it; I choose to ignore this, and settle into a seat. At Langogne I rent a bicycle at the SNCF station; I've telephoned in advance to reserve it, I've organized things well. Then I get on the bike, and am instantly aware of the absurdity of the project: it's ten years since I've done any cycling, Saint-Cirgues is forty kilometres away, the road there is very mountainous and I feel barely capable of covering two kilometres on the flat. I've lost all aptitude, and what's more all appetite, for physical effort.

The road will be permanent torture, but rather abstract, if you can say that. The region is totally deserted; you penetrate deeper and deeper into the mountains. I suffer, I've dramatically over-estimated my physical reserves. And the final goal of the journey no longer seems so wonderful, it becomes more nebulous as I ascend these unavailing and endless gradients without even looking at the landscape.

Right in the middle of one difficult climb, as I'm gasping like an asphyxiated canary, I spot a sign: 'Caution. Shot-firing'. Despite everything, I find it a little hard to believe. Who'd be after me here?

The explanation dawns on me a little while later. In fact the sign refers to quarrying; it's only rocks, then, that are to be destroyed. I like that better.

The going gets flatter; I raise my head. To the right of the road there is a hill of rubble, midway between dust and small pebbles. The sloping surface is grey, of a geometric and absolute flatness. Very enticing. I'm sure if you set foot there you'd sink straight down for several metres.

From time to time I stop beside the road, I smoke a cigarette, I shed a few tears and then I press on. I wish I were dead. But 'there is a road to travel, and it must be travelled.'

I arrive at Saint-Cirgues in a pathetic state of exhaustion and I make for the *Parfum des Bois* hotel. After a short rest I go and drink a beer in the hotel bar. The people of the village have a friendly and welcoming air; they bid me good day.

I hope no one is going to engage me in conversation of a more precise kind, ask me if I'm doing a spot of tourism, where I've come from by bike, if I find the region to my taste, etc. But happily none of this occurs.

My margin of manoeuvre in life has become singularly restricted. I still envisage a number of possibilities, but they vary only in points of detail.

The dinner will settle nothing. Still, I've taken three Tercians in the meantime. And here I am, alone at my table, I've asked for the gastronomic menu. It is absolutely delicious; even the wine is good. I cry while eating, emitting little sobs.

Later, in my room, I will try and sleep; once more in vain. The sad cerebral routine; the passing of a night that seems frozen in time; the images that are disbursed with increasing parsimony. Whole minutes to straighten the bedspread.

Around four in the morning, though, the night takes on a different cast. Something is stirring deep within, asking to be revealed. The very nature of this journey is undergoing a change: in my mind it becomes something decisive, almost heroic.

On 21 June, around seven, I get up, have my breakfast and leave by bike for the Forest of Mazan. Yesterday's hearty dinner has had the effect of giving me renewed strength; I ride supply, effortlessly, through the pines.

The weather is wonderfully fine, pleasant, springlike. The Forest of Mazan is very pretty and also profoundly reassuring. It is a real country forest. There are gently rising paths, clearings, a sun which penetrates everywhere. The meadows are covered in daffodils. One feels content, happy; there are no people. Something seems possible, here. One has the impression of being present at a new departure.

And of a sudden all this evaporates. A great mental shock restores me to the deepest part of myself. And I take stock, and I ironize, but at the same time I have respect for myself. What a capacity I have for grandiose mental images, and of seeing them through! How clear, once more, is the image I have of the world! The richness of what is dying inside me is absolutely prodigious; I needn't feel ashamed of myself; I shall have tried.

I stretch out in a meadow, in the sun. And now it hurts, lying down in this softest of meadows, in the midst of this most amiable and reassuring of landscapes. Everything which might have been a source of pleasure, of participation, of innocent sensual harmony, has become a source of suffering and unhappiness. At the same time I feel, and with impressive violence, the possibility of joy. For years I have been walking alongside a phantom who looks like me, and who lives in a theoretical paradise strictly related to the world. I've long believed that it was up to me to become one with this phantom. That's done with.

I cycle still further into the forest. On the other side of that hill is the source of the River Ardèche, the map says. The fact no longer interests me; I continue nevertheless. And I no longer even know where the source is; at present, everything looks the same. The landscape is more and more gentle, amiable, joyous; my skin hurts. I am at the heart of the abyss. I feel my skin again as a frontier, and the external world as a crushing weight. The impression of separation is total; from now on I am imprisoned within myself. It will not take place, the sublime fusion; the goal of life is missed. It is two in the afternoon.